Books in the Replica series

1: Amy, Number 7
2: Pursuing Amy
3: Another Amy

Look out for:

4: Perfect Girls
5: Secret Clique
6: And the Two Shall Meet
7: The Best of the Best

Book 3

Another Amy

Marilyn Kaye

Hodder
Children's
Books

a division of Hodder Headline

Copyright © 1999 by Marilyn Kaye

First published as a Bantam Skylark paperback in the
USA in 1998 by Bantam, Doubleday Dell
Publishing Group Inc, USA

This paperback edition published in Great Britain in 2000
by Hodder Children's Books

10 9 8 7 6 5 4 3 2 1

A Catalogue record for this book
is available from the British Library

ISBN 0340 74953 9

Typeset by Hewer Text Ltd, Edinburgh
Printed and bound in Great Britain by
Clays Ltd, St Ives plc

Hodder Children's Books
A Division of Hodder Headline
338 Euston Road
London NW1 3BH

For my ally and friend, Samantha Wylde Lang

Memo from the Director

RECENT REPORTS INDICATE THE EXISTENCE OF THREE
POTENTIAL SUBJECTS OF INTEREST TO THE ORGANI-
SATION. IT HAS BEEN SUGGESTED THAT THE INVES-
TIGATIVE COMMITTEE SHIFT THE FOCUS FROM THE
ORIGINAL SUBJECT AND CONSIDER THE POSSIBILITY
THAT EQUALLY VIABLE SOURCES ARE AVAILABLE. ALL
AVENUES OF DISCOVERY SHOULD BE EXPLORED IN
PURSUIT OF THE ULTIMATE GOAL. THUS, IT IS
STRONGLY RECOMMENDED THAT THE ORGANISATION
EXTEND THE PARAMETERS OF THE STUDY.

1

At Parkside Middle School, the noise level in the halls was deafening: the last bell of the day was still ringing, students were yelling, locker doors were slamming, and three hundred pairs of feet were racing to the exit. Despite all this, Amy Candler was able to hear Tasha Morgan call to her from the other end of the hall.

She looked up. Tasha was pretty far away, but Amy could read the expression on her best friend's face. Something was up.

When Tasha came close enough to hear *her*, Amy asked, 'What's going on? Aren't you going to gymnastics today?'

Tasha nodded, but Amy knew that the smile on her face had nothing to do with vaults and uneven parallel bars. 'I had to see you before I left. Guess what?'

Amy rolled her eyes. Why did people ask you to 'guess what?' when you had no idea what they were talking about? She might have certain special abilities and skills, but mind-reading wasn't one of them. Still, she made a stab at a guess. 'You've gone up another bra size.'

Now it was Tasha's turn to do some eye rolling. 'No.'

'Okay, what?'

'I'm going to be a newspaper reporter.'

Amy's brow furrowed. 'For the *Snooze*?' She was referring to the school's weekly newspaper, and she couldn't understand why Tasha would be excited about that. Anyone could write for the *Snooze*, and no one wanted to — it was the most boring newspaper on earth.

'No! For the *Journal*!'

Amy was impressed. 'The *Journal*? The paper we get at home? Wow, that's a *real* newspaper.'

Tasha nodded happily. 'I'm the new Parkside Middle School contributor. Actually, I'm the first. The paper just started a programme where they have a reporter from each school in the district. My English teacher recommended me.'

'Cool,' Amy said. 'That's great, Tasha, congratulations.' She knew this had to be a big deal, and she would have hugged Tasha, but that wasn't cool. It certainly wasn't the kind of thing you did in a crowded school hallway. Not that Amy was concerned with being cool, but she wasn't in the habit of calling attention to herself. 'What are you going to write about?' she asked.

The joy on Tasha's face faded a little. 'I don't know. Coming up with something interesting is going to be the challenge.'

'What about the cheerleading tryouts this month? You could cover that.'

'I guess,' Tasha said without enthusiasm. 'But that's the kind of thing the other school reporters will write about. I want to write something different, something that makes a splash.'

'You could interview the new gym teacher,' Amy suggested. 'Wasn't he on an Olympic track team?'

'Yeah, about a hundred years ago, and he fell in the first lap. That's why he's a gym teacher.' Tasha cocked her head thoughtfully. 'But an interview

. . . that's not a bad idea. If I could think of someone really interesting, someone different, someone who's not like anyone else . . .' She gazed up at the ceiling with a very innocent, thoughtful expression.

Amy's eyes narrowed in suspicion. 'Someone like who?'

'Oh, maybe a twelve-year-old girl with exceptional powers. A girl who's recently discovered that she's a' – Tasha lowered her voice – 'human clone. What makes her different from other people, how she feels about herself. Now, that could be an absolutely awesome interview.'

'Maybe,' Amy said. 'But not for me.' She wasn't alarmed at Tasha's hints. She knew she could trust her.

'I was just kidding. You don't have to worry, your secret is safe with me. I'll never tell anyone,' Tasha vowed, as if to assure Amy that her faith was justified.

'I know,' Amy said. 'That's why I told you.'

'And I should have been the *only* person you told,' Tasha remarked. 'I still don't understand why Eric has to know. And you told him *first*! I can't believe you did that.'

'Get over it,' Amy said cheerfully. She knew Tasha wasn't happy about sharing Amy's secret with her brother, but there wasn't anything Amy could do about that. And Tasha knew perfectly well why Eric had learned about the secret first. 'Good grief, Tasha, some creep was chasing me. We were in danger! I couldn't make Eric run for his life without telling him why!'

'Yeah, I guess that makes sense,' Tasha said grudgingly. 'He was just there. It's not like you planned to tell him first.'

'Of course not,' Amy assured her. Not that she minded sharing her secret with Tasha's older brother. She'd harboured a secret crush on him for ages — and lately she'd begun to think that the feeling just might be mutual. He'd started catching up with her and Tasha on their walk to school most mornings. He usually passed her locker on his way out of school, and sometimes he walked home with them, too, if he didn't have basketball or track practice. She hadn't seen him today, though.

'Where *is* Eric, anyway?' she asked, trying not to sound too terribly interested.

'Detention,' Tasha told her. 'He was late this morning.'

'Oh, right.' She'd been disappointed when he didn't catch up with her and Tasha on their way to school.

On the other hand, Tasha wasn't at all pleased by the fact that Eric had been hanging out with them. 'That's why we actually had some time alone,' she said pointedly. Then she snapped her fingers. 'I remembered the name of that commercial I saw on TV. It was for Sunshine Orange Juice.'

'What are you talking about?'

'The commercial with the girl who looks exactly like you. It was during the six o'clock news on Channel Four.'

'Come on, Tasha,' Amy groaned. Tasha was seeing Amy clones everywhere lately. The last one had been a face in a blurry newspaper photo of science fair winners, and the only thing she had in common with Amy was her sex and the length of her hair.

'Honestly, Amy, you should watch the Channel Four news tonight; the same commercial might be on. I swear, this girl could be another—'

'Shhh,' Amy hissed. Jeanine Bryant was heading their way.

'Tasha!' Jeanine called. 'Hurry up, my mother's

out front. We've been waiting for you!' She and Tasha took gymnastics at the same place, and their mothers had organised a car pool, much to Tasha's dismay. She didn't like Jeanine any more than Amy did.

And now that Jeanine saw Amy with Tasha, she wasn't in such a rush to get back to her mother's car. 'Did you get your essay back today in English?' she asked Amy.

'Of course,' Amy replied. 'We *all* got our essays back. And before you ask, yes, I got an A. I suppose you got an A, too.'

'Mmm. But I was wondering if the teacher wrote a note on your paper,' Jeanine said casually.

'You mean like "very good"?'

Jeanine smiled in her most annoyingly triumphant way. 'Mine said "excellent." Come on, Tasha.'

Tasha paused to offer Amy an apologetic shrug before running after Jeanine towards the exit. Watching them leave, Amy had no desire to go with them, but she still felt a little abandoned. Up until a few months ago, she had taken gymnastics, too. Then her special talents had kicked in. She could suddenly do complicated, twisting back flips

7

on the balance beam and uneven parallel bars. And that was just the beginning . . .

Coach Persky had been so impressed that he'd wanted to start training her for national competition. Her mother had refused – in fact, she'd become so alarmed by Amy's extraordinary talent that she'd made her daughter quit. Becoming a world-class gymnast was the kind of publicity Amy didn't need.

The crowd in the hall had thinned out considerably. Amy had nothing else to do at school, but she didn't hurry to leave. Instead, she walked in the opposite direction, towards the administrative offices. She'd never had detention herself, but she knew that the unfortunate ones who did had to sign in at the principal's office before they went to the cafeteria-jail, and they had to sign out when they left. She just hoped Eric had only been sentenced to the minimum of twenty minutes.

When she got to the principal's office, Amy paused outside the door. The secretary was busy stacking a pile of neon blue papers on her desk. Then Amy saw what she was looking for: a clipboard with the list of students in detention that day. The list wasn't too long, and it was facing her.

Standing up on her toes, she leaned into the door-way without being seen and focused her eyes on the list. There it was – *Eric Morgan*. He hadn't signed out yet.

Amy was about to leave when the secretary turned to the photocopier. She watched as the woman pressed the On button and more neon blue papers shot out. Amy knew colourful paper was used only for important memos and wondered what was up. A normal person wouldn't be able to read the pages that were pouring out of the machine – they were too far away, and coming out too fast. But Amy wasn't a normal person. She focused her eyes even more intently this time.

TO ALL TEACHERS: *Please be advised that personnel from Electra Entertainment will be on the school grounds over the next two weeks to film scenes for the upcoming movie* Middle School Maniac. *All efforts will be made to ensure that classes are not disrupted. However, there may be some inconveniences, and if this is the case, you are advised to remember that Electra Entertainment is making a substantial contribution to the school renovation fund in appreciation for the use of our facilities. You are also advised to refrain from informing the students as to the nature and purpose of our visitors, so as to avoid distracting them from their studies.*

Amy tried to imagine an explanation teachers could give for the presence of movie cameras and all the accompanying equipment without telling students what was really going on. She couldn't think of one.

'Hey, what are you doing here?'

Amy whirled around. It was Eric. She hoped her face wasn't going pink. Unfortunately, her special talents did not extend to creative lying.

'Oh, I was just, you know, doing, um, something . . .'

Happily, Eric didn't really seem to care why she was there. 'You going home now? Hang on, I have to sign out; then I'll walk with you.'

Amy feigned nonchalance. 'How was detention?' she asked him as they walked out, and then she immediately wanted to kick herself for asking such a stupid question. But Eric didn't seem to mind.

'The usual. You just sit there and read or stare into space. I'll bet you've never had detention.'

She had to admit he was right.

'I've had detention three times so far this year,' Eric said.

'Really?' Amy wasn't sure whether she should act shocked or impressed.

'It was only for being tardy,' he added hastily. 'Not for fighting or anything serious.' He grinned. 'I'll bet that's something you never have to worry about. Being tardy.'

'Oh, I've been known to oversleep,' Amy assured him.

'Yeah, but your legs are like speeding bullets. Bet you can get to school in about two minutes, right?'

Amy shrugged. She didn't have the slightest idea what her top running speed was; she'd never tested herself. And she didn't want to exaggerate her skills. 'Not in two minutes. I can run pretty fast, but it's not like I've got real superpowers, like a comic-book hero. I can't fly, and I can't see through walls. Unless they're made of glass,' she added, as a little joke. 'I'm only human.'

'Right. I guess you are.'

Was he disappointed in her now? She tried to make up for it. 'Of course, I can see farther than most people, and I can hear better. And I can read really fast. Like just now, when I was standing outside the principal's office.' She told him what she'd seen coming out of the photo-copy machine.

'No kidding? They're making a movie at Park-side? Are there going to be big movie stars hanging out?'

'I don't know, the note didn't say. I think they're trying to keep the whole thing secret.'

'I won't tell anyone,' he assured her.

As they walked, their hands kept accidentally banging into each other. Or maybe it wasn't by accident. In any case, it seemed perfectly natural to suddenly find themselves holding hands. Of course, they both pretended not to notice that this was happening.

'Have you ever thought about what you could do?' Eric asked.

'Huh?'

'With all your superior abilities, I mean. You can do things better than other people, like seeing and hearing and remembering stuff. And you're stron-ger and faster. You could be a major Olympic athlete. Or you could go on that quiz show where you have to remember what you saw in a square and match it with another square. You could make a fortune.'

She just shrugged.

'Or you could be a poker champion,' he continued.

'I don't know how to play poker.'

'I could teach you sometime.'

'Okay.'

There was a moment of silence.

'You know Ronald Hurley?' Eric asked.

Amy was startled. The question had come out of no-where. 'Ronald Hurley,' she repeated.

'He lives around the corner from us. Red hair, my age, shorter than me. He always wears purple high-tops.'

'Oh, sure,' Amy said. 'Between the hair and the sneakers, he's pretty colourful.'

Eric laughed. 'Well, we're both playing Disaster Isle. You know, the computer game? He told me he's reached level eight.' Eric sounded annoyed. 'I'm only at level five, and I've had the game for a month. He only got it last week.'

'He must be really smart,' Amy commented.

'Not *that* smart,' Eric said. 'Personally, I think he's lying.'

'Oh.' She didn't know what he wanted her to say.

'The thing is . . .,' he began slowly, and then the words came out in a rush. 'It would be easy for you to see into the Hurleys' den from the street. That's where Ronald keeps his computer. He uses it every day.'

'Possibly,' Amy acknowledged.

'I was thinking . . . you could casually stroll by and look when he's playing Disaster Isle. See if he really is on level eight. Because if he's not, I could challenge him to a game and everyone would know he's been lying.'

Amy was startled. 'You want me to *spy* on Ronald Hurley?'

Eric nodded.

Well, it wasn't exactly illegal. 'I guess I could do that,' she said, a bit reluctantly.

Eric grinned and squeezed her hand warmly. 'That's great!'

'No problem.'

But she couldn't help wondering if Eric would have been this happy with her if she hadn't had special powers – if she'd been just a regular, normal, ordinary twelve-year-old girl.

If she hadn't been a human being whose DNA structure had been artificially engineered. A biological entity created by a group of scientists from the most superior genetic material in the universe.

2

'Tell Tasha to call me when she gets home,' Amy told Eric when they reached the condo community where they both lived.

'Okay,' he replied. He gave her an abashed grin, and she smiled back, because they both knew it was very likely he'd forget to give Tasha the message. Unlike Amy, Eric didn't have a particularly great memory.

It didn't matter anyway. Amy and Tasha talked on the phone every night, and neither of them needed a reminder to call. Despite seeing each other every day, they always had something new to talk about.

At this very moment, though, Amy wanted to talk to her mother about something she couldn't discuss with Tasha. Nancy Candler was a professor at the university, where she taught biology, but she didn't have any Monday classes this term, so she usually worked at home, grading papers. Today she wasn't alone. Their neighbour, Monica Jackson, was in the kitchen with Nancy, and the two women were drinking coffee when Amy walked in.

'Hi, honey,' Nancy greeted her, and Monica added a cheery salute. Amy flopped down at the kitchen table and grabbed a chocolate-chip cookie. After one bite, her eyes widened.

'Wow, Mom, these are outstanding!'

'Don't thank me,' Nancy said. 'Monica brought them.'

Monica amended that. 'I didn't just bring them, I *made* them.'

Amy tried not to look too surprised. Monica was hardly the domestic type. She was an artist and often seemed to consider herself a canvas. Her hair was her hobby; it went through periodic colour and style changes. It was currently green, and so was her fingernail polish. To accentuate all this green, she was wearing huge chunks of jade jewellery and a long, flowing dress that resembled an Indian sari. Sometimes she could look pretty bizarre, but Amy admired her guts – it was clear that she didn't care what anyone else thought of her.

'I used three kinds of chocolate in these cookies,' Monica pointed out. 'I'm trying to come up with new and exciting chocolate treats.'

'Why?' Amy asked.

Monica laughed. 'Why else? I'm going out with a chocoholic!'

This was the perfect lead-in to the discussion Amy wanted to have. 'So you think this guy will fall madly in love with you if you give him chocolate? I guess that could happen. Don't they say the way to a man's heart is through his stomach?'

'I don't know,' Monica said. 'Sometimes I think the only way to a man's heart is with a scalpel.'

'Now, Monica,' Nancy reproved her. 'Don't be so cynical. Not all men are scum.' She sighed. 'Just some of them.'

'Like that Brad Carrington you were going out with,' Monica said. 'You never told me why you two stopped seeing each other. It was just before you got so sick with that mysterious illness, right? The doctors never found out what made you fall into that coma, did they?'

'No.'

'Maybe it was Brad that made you so sick,' Monica remarked. Amy knew she was kidding, of course, but Monica had no idea how close to the truth she was getting.

'I don't understand guys at all,' Amy announced.

'Guys in general?' her mother asked. 'Or one guy in particular?' She knew how Amy felt about Eric.

Amy tried to explain. 'With my friends, girl-friends I mean, I can usually tell how they're feeling. You know, if they're happy, or angry, or depressed, or whatever. With guys, it's different. I can't figure out how they feel.'

She watched as Nancy and Monica gave each other knowing looks. Clearly, she wasn't alone in this.

'I wish I could give you some profound advice,' Nancy said. 'But I'm not exactly the most experi-enced woman when it comes to men.'

'At least you've been married,' Monica pointed out. 'That automatically makes you more experi-enced than I am.'

Amy and her mother glanced at each other quickly, and then just as quickly averted their eyes. Amy knew that Nancy had to be thinking what she was thinking – that there was a lot Monica didn't know about them.

Like all their friends and acquaintances, Monica thought that Nancy was a widow who had married a man named Steve Anderson thirteen years earlier, and that he had been killed in an accident just months before their daughter, Amy, was born. That was the standard story Nancy gave out when she had to explain her situation. She even had a photo of this Steve Anderson, a guy she had known vaguely during her college days and who had died at the right time. It was unlikely Monica would ever know that Nancy had never had a husband – and that Amy had never had a father.

'Speaking of men,' Monica said, rising, 'I've got one coming over for dinner, and I'd better get started.'

'Cooking?' Nancy asked.

'No,' Monica replied. 'Deciding what restaurant I'll order a delivery from. Which I will then arrange on my own platters and let him think I've been slaving in the kitchen all day.' She noticed the pendant hanging on Amy's neck and touched it. 'That's pretty. It's a crescent moon, isn't it?' Monica made very artistic jewellery, and she was always interested in unusual pieces. 'It's a nice design. Where did you get it?'

The question startled Amy, and for a moment her mind went blank. Finally she said, 'It was a gift.'

'From a cousin,' her mother added.

As soon as Monica had left, Nancy gave Amy an understanding smile. 'It's not easy to keep secrets, is it?'

'No.' Nancy was gazing at her searchingly, so Amy added, 'I haven't told anyone else, Mom. Just Tasha and Eric.'

Nancy nodded, but she let out a small sigh. 'I still wish you hadn't told either of them, Amy.'

'Tasha and Eric won't ever tell a soul,' Amy assured her.

'I know they wouldn't betray you, not consciously,' Nancy said. 'But one of them could slip up. They're only human.'

'And I'm not,' Amy muttered.

'Don't say that,' Nancy said sharply. 'You *are* human, Amy. You're just . . . well, you're special. And all I'm saying is that sometimes people with the best intentions can say things they don't mean to say.'

Nancy was right; Amy knew that. Still, she didn't

regret telling her two closest friends her big secret. 'I just have to have someone to talk to, someone who can understand why I'm different. I know I've got you, Mom,' she added quickly, 'and it was okay when I had you and Dr J. But now he's gone.' Her eyes filled up automatically, the way they always did when she remembered the kind man who had been Nancy's boss, the head of Project Crescent and the person who, more than anyone, had understood what made Amy tick. He'd died only a few weeks earlier, and not from natural causes.

Amy fingered her pendant. Dr Jaleski had created it for her – making jewellery had been his hobby. After his death, his daughter, Mary, had delivered it to Amy. She'd said that her father wanted Amy to have it so she'd never forget who she was. As if she could.

'You *are* being very careful, aren't you?' Nancy asked anxiously.

'Are *you*?' Amy countered.

To anyone else's ears, that would have sounded like a very rude retort for a daughter to make to her mother. But Nancy knew what Amy was referring to, and she made a face. 'Brad seemed so normal. Better than normal. You can't really blame me for being taken in.'

'He had me fooled, too, Mom,' Amy said comfortingly. But she gave an involuntary shudder as she recalled Brad Carrington, her mother's ex-boyfriend. He'd been so good-looking and personable. Nancy had met him at an art gallery opening. At the time, it had seemed like a happy accident. Later Nancy and Amy had realised that the encounter must have been planned well in advance. Because in the end, they'd discovered that Amy was Brad's real motivation in his romantic pursuit of Nancy.

He had been one of *them*, a member of the mysterious government agency that had funded Project Crescent. The scientists involved had thought they were working on a project that would eradicate genetic disorders. Too late they'd learned that their mission was to create a master race of genetically superior humans – a frightening goal. So the scientists had taken it upon themselves to destroy the project by blowing up their lab. But the secret agency, the organisation, still existed, and Brad was connected to it. Amy and Nancy had learned the truth almost too late.

Nancy was clearly thinking along the same lines. She reached out and took her daughter's hand.

'You saved my life,' she said. 'How many mothers can say that to their daughters?'

'You saved *my* life,' Amy pointed out. 'So now we're even.' The two hugged each other, and Amy knew both of them were hoping they'd never have to save each other again. But that could be wishful thinking. Events had convinced them that the organisation didn't believe all the clones had perished in the explosion. They wanted information. They wanted Amy – or someone just like her.

At least Amy felt pretty certain they wouldn't kill her, not like they'd killed Dr Jaleski. They wanted her alive.

When her mother released her, Amy let out a yawn.

'Tired?' Nancy asked.

'A little,' Amy admitted. 'I didn't get much sleep last night.'

Concern crossed her mother's face. 'Have you been having that dream again?' She didn't need to be any more specific than that. In Amy's nightmare, she was trapped under glass, and there was fire raging all around her. At the last minute, she was rescued. And it was all the more horrifying because it had really happened.

24

'I haven't had that dream for a while,' she told her mother. 'Maybe that's because I know what it means now.' She yawned again. 'I was up late reading,' she confessed. 'I borrowed a great mystery from Tasha and I can't put it down.'

Nancy laughed. 'Now, Amy, I know perfectly well that you can read a two-hundred-page book in less than thirty minutes.'

'Yeah, but it's more fun to read like a regular person,' Amy said. She went to the refrigerator and looked inside. 'Can I have a Coke?'

'I suppose so,' Nancy said, 'but I wish you wouldn't drink so much soda. It's bad for your teeth. Did you know that if you put a perfectly healthy tooth in a glass of cola, it will dissolve in seventy-two hours?'

Amy looked at her mother in exasperation. 'Come on, Mom, nothing's going to hurt *my* teeth.' She'd never had a dental problem in her life. She'd never had the measles, the mumps, the chickenpox, the flu . . . she'd never even had a fever. That was the number-one benefit of having been created from the best possible genetic material – no illness.

Amy took her Coke upstairs to her room and turned on her computer. She checked her e-mail, even though she wasn't expecting anything, and so wasn't surprised when the mailbox was empty. Still, she had fantasies of someday clicking on the e-mail icon and discovering that someone was looking for her, the way she was looking for other Amys.

When Nancy and the other scientists had decided to destroy Project Crescent, they couldn't bring themselves to destroy the infant clones they had produced. So they'd planned to secretly remove the clones from the laboratory and send them all over the world to be adopted and hopefully brought up by normal parents as normal children, never to know they were different.

Of the twelve Amys, the last to be removed was Number Seven. It was while Number Seven was still in her incubator that the explosive device had gone off prematurely. Nancy Candler had run into the laboratory to save Amy Number Seven. Some sort of emotional bonding had taken place in that rescue, and she'd taken this Amy home to raise as her own.

But Nancy didn't know – or at least, she *claimed* not to know – where the others were. They were out there somewhere: twelve-year-old girls with brown hair and brown eyes and the mark of a crescent moon like a small tattoo on their right shoulder. Of course, it was impossible to know whether or not they had discovered what they were, the way Amy Number Seven ultimately had.

Amy had seen one of her clones once. It was during a performance of *The Nutcracker* by a touring ballet company from France. When Amy had spotted the dancer who played Marie, it had been like looking in a mirror. According to the programme, the dancer's name was Annie Perrault.

Amy's attempts to speak to Annie after the performance had failed. Now she didn't want to go too far in her efforts to locate her. Amy knew the organisation was aware of *her* existence. She didn't want to put Annie Perrault in danger, too.

Later that evening, Amy wanted to clear her mind and went for a walk around the complex. As she absently went by Ronald Hurley's house, Amy remembered Eric's request and realised that he was right. She could see directly into the Hurleys' den from the street. In fact, now that she was looking, she recognised the boy, just before the light in the room went off. She wouldn't be able to read his computer screen now.

She wasn't sure she even wanted to. The idea of using her skills to spy on some innocent person didn't seem particularly ethical. She had a pretty good feeling she'd end up telling Eric to forget it.

Or maybe she wouldn't have to. With his memory, Eric would more than likely forget he'd even asked her for the favour.

3

On the way to school the next morning, Amy was pleased to note that Eric would not be receiving detention for tardiness that day. She and Tasha were already several blocks from home, but she could distinctly hear Eric yelling, 'Bye, Mom,' and the slam of the door as he left the house.

'Eric's coming,' she announced, knowing that Tasha couldn't have heard anything. Tasha made a gagging sound, her standard response to any mention of her brother's name.

Eric was on the school track team, so he was a pretty fast runner for someone with ordinary genes. It was only a couple of minutes before he caught up with them.

'Are the movie stars going to be there today?' he asked Amy.

'I don't know. The memo didn't say exactly when they were coming.'

'What movie stars?' Tasha asked. 'What memo?'

Amy told her about seeing the notice coming out of the photocopier in the principal's office the day before. 'It's called *Middle School Maniac*, so I guess it's a horror film. It's funny how many scary movies take place in schools.'

'That's because schools are scary places,' Eric said. 'Most of the movies are about high schools. I've never seen one set in a middle school before.'

'They've probably trying to appeal to a younger audience,' Tasha decided. 'Why didn't you tell me about this last night?'

Eric spoke before Amy could. 'Because it's a big secret. The memo said teachers shouldn't tell us students because we'd get too distracted. I guess it would really freak them out if we ever got excited about something.'

'How do you know so much about this?' Tasha asked her brother.

He nodded towards Amy. 'She told me.'

Just then, from a distance, a male voice bellowed,

'Yo, Morgan!' Eric turned and waved at two boys half a block away. 'I gotta see those guys.' He took off to join his friends.

Tasha turned to Amy. 'It's a secret? And you told *Eric*?' She looked surprised, and a little hurt. 'You told Eric and not me?'

'He was there when I saw the memo,' Amy said. 'I meant to tell you. I guess I forgot.'

A flicker of doubt crossed Tasha's face. Then she frowned. 'I can't believe you told Eric something you don't want the entire universe to know. He's got a big mouth.'

'Oh, Tasha, that's not true. I can trust Eric to keep a secret.' Amy turned to look back at him with his buddies. They had their heads together, and they were laughing. She supposed that if she concentrated, she could hear what they were talking about, but she never felt right eavesdropping. Besides, what could they be laughing about that she would want to know?

'Eric can keep a secret,' she said again. Tasha just shrugged. She was still clearly a little annoyed that Eric knew something about Amy that she hadn't known first.

It was while she was on her way to lunch three

and a half hours later that Amy got the first indication that her trust in Eric might be misplaced. The door of a girls' rest room opened as she passed, and she caught a snippet of conversation.

'Wouldn't it be so amazing if there's someone fabulous in the movie? Like Leonardo DiCaprio or Brad Pitt? Or the guy who killed everyone in *Scream*? The first one, not the second.'

Of course, the girls could have been talking about a movie they were planning to see that coming weekend. But Amy's fears were confirmed when she joined the line at the cafeteria. The two boys in front of her were talking.

'I think Demi Moore's in it.'

'No way, she's too old to be in middle school.'

'She could be playing a teacher.'

Amy was scowling by the time she reached the table where Tasha was already seated. She slammed her tray down.

'What's the matter?' Tasha asked.

Before Amy could tell her, two girls from their American history class sat down at the table. 'I wonder if any of us will get to be in it,' one of them said to the other.

'I'll bet they'll need extras,' the other one said.

Amy pretended to be confused. 'What are you guys talking about?'

'The movie! Didn't you hear about it? They're making a movie right here at Parkside.'

'Who told you that?' Amy demanded.

'It's all over school,' the girl said. 'Everyone knows about it, Amy. Where have you been?'

Aghast, Amy looked at Tasha, who nodded wisely. 'I *told* you he wouldn't be able to keep it a secret.'

Amy sank back in her chair. She couldn't believe it – but it was so obviously true. On the way to school, Eric must have told his friends about the movie. Those two friends could have spread the word in their home-rooms. Those classmates could have passed the message to friends in second period, who would then have moved on to third period . . . yes, it was easy to see how the news could have gotten all over school by lunch-time.

The shock passed, and anger took its place. How could Eric do this to her? She'd made it very clear that this was a secret, that she was sharing the news with him and him alone.

At least Tasha was sympathetic. 'Don't worry

about it,' she advised. 'Everyone would have found out sooner or later.'

'Yeah, I guess so. But that's not the point.' Amy leaned forward so only Tasha could hear her. 'If I can't trust Eric with *that* secret . . .'

She didn't need to say more. Tasha understood what Amy was implying. She shook her head almost violently and actually defended her brother.

'Oh, no, he would never tell anyone about' – she lowered her voice to a whisper – '*that*. He knows how dangerous it would be for you. This movie thing isn't a really important secret. And no one will be able to trace it back to you. You won't get into any trouble.'

That was true, but it didn't make Amy feel any better. After all, a secret was a secret, and as far as she was concerned, you could either trust someone or you couldn't. Apparently, Eric couldn't be trusted. And that really saddened her. When she spotted him coming out of the cafeteria line, she hurried over and cornered him before he reached his table.

'I can't believe you did that!' she snapped.

'Huh?'

'I told you it was a secret, Eric! And you went and blabbed to everyone!'

34

'What are you talking about?' The lack of comprehension on his face was almost believable.

'The movie! Everyone at school knows there's going to be a movie made here and it's because you can't keep a secret!'

'I didn't tell anyone about the movie,' he said indignantly.

Amy gave him the harshest look she could muster up. 'Oh, *please*! I'm no fool. You and Tasha were the only people I told, and I know Tasha would never reveal a secret. I just hope you don't plan on telling people any other secrets of mine!' With that, she whirled around and went back to her table. She didn't sit down, though. She had completely lost her appetite.

'I'm going to the rest room,' she told Tasha. Tasha didn't offer to join her. She could tell when Amy wanted to be alone.

But Amy hadn't been in the rest room for more than fifteen seconds before the door swung open. And the last person she wanted to see at that moment – or at any moment – sauntered in.

Jeanine went directly to a mirror, examining herself with an intensity that was unusual even for someone as vain as she was. Then she turned to Amy with a thin, forced smile and an expression Amy knew too well: Jeanine was about to regale her with a new accomplishment.

'I'm going to be in the movie,' she announced.

'What?'

'*Middle School Maniac*. Haven't you heard about it? It's going to be filmed right here at Parkside. And I'm going to have a part in it.'

Amy looked at her sceptically. Jeanine was pretty, she had to admit that; but while Amy didn't know anything about show business, she was sure you couldn't just waltz up to the director and get a part. 'I don't think you should count on that, Jeanine. I heard we're not supposed to bother the movie people.'

Jeanine continued to display her nasty little smile. '*You're* not supposed to bother the movie people. But, see, my father's bank is investing in this film, and the producer had dinner at our house on Sunday. He said he'd tell the director to give me a part.'

At this point, Amy half-expected Jeanine to stick out her tongue and say, 'So there,' but they were practically teenagers now, so Jeanine managed to control herself. Since Amy had no particular interest in a film career, Jeanine's announcement wasn't unnerving. But a thought struck her.

'Wait a minute . . . this means you knew about the movie last weekend.'

'Oh, I've known about it for ages,' Jeanine said airily.

'And you probably told everyone you knew.'

'Not everyone,' Jeanine replied. 'Just my friends.' And with a look that added, 'Of which you are not one,' she sauntered out of the rest room.

Amy felt unbelievably small and stupid. She counted to five, to give Jeanine time to get farther away from the rest room, and then tore out and headed back to the cafeteria. She knew better than to go directly to where Eric was sitting. A seventh-grade girl didn't march over to a table where half a dozen ninth-grade boys were grouped together. Eric would just be embarrassed, and his friends would tease him mercilessly.

Since there were only a few minutes left in the lunch period, she waited in the hall and waved to Eric as he emerged. She wasn't at all surprised when he seemed less than thrilled to see her.

'What's the matter *now*?' he asked.

Amy was appropriately humble. 'I owe you an

apology. I was wrong. It wasn't you who let every-one know about the movie.'

'That's what I told you,' Eric said. 'But you didn't believe me.'

'I'm really, sorry,' Amy said.

'Yeah, whatever.' Abruptly he turned away and stalked off.

'What was that all about?'

Amy turned to find Tasha behind her. 'It was Jeanine who spread the rumour about the movie, not Eric. So I apologised, but I think he's pretty mad at me.'

Tasha shrugged. 'He'll get over it. Eric thinks—'

A shout from the end of the hall cut her off. Amy didn't need superior hearing to find out what was going on.

'They're here!' someone shrieked. 'The movie people!'

At least a dozen kids, Amy and Tasha among them, raced to the windows. Two stretch limou-sines, three trucks, and four huge mobile homes pulled into the school parking lot.

The sound of three bells indicated that a message was about to come through the intercom. 'Boys and girls, please go to your next-period class immedi-ately. Do not linger in the halls.'

'They must have spies out here,' Tasha grumbled as she took one last peek out the window before starting towards the stairs. 'Amy, I've got to meet those movie people.'

'Why?' Amy asked.

'For the *Journal*! This could be my chance to write something really different. What it's like when movie stars invade an ordinary school. And maybe I could interview the director and the stars. I could get a whole series out of this! What do you think?'

'Could be pretty awesome,' Amy admitted. 'But how are you going to get near the filming? I'm sure they'll have guards all over the place keeping us mere students far away.'

'I've got press credentials,' Tasha said importantly. 'Look.' She took a card from her wallet that stated that Tasha Morgan was a legitimate representative of *The Parkside Journal*.

To Amy's eyes, it didn't look very official. 'It doesn't even have a photo.'

'It's a temporary card, until I have a chance to go to the newspaper office and have a picture taken. Hey, you want to come with me? I could say you're my assistant or something.'

Amy seriously doubted that any guard would accept the notion that a middle school student would have an assistant, but it wouldn't hurt to try, and it could be fun to see how a movie got made. 'Yeah, okay.'

'Meet me at my locker after the last bell,' Tasha said, and the girls separated to go to their classes.

Tasha was nervous.

'I'm so glad you're coming with me,' she said as Amy joined her by her locker that afternoon. They headed towards the exit. 'Like, what if they start yelling at me to get out of there or something?'

'You're a journalist,' Amy pointed out. 'Journalists have to go to a lot of places where they're not welcome.'

But once outside, even Amy felt a little uneasy. The largest mobile home was parked just in front of the school, and there were three big men hovering around it. Several students were hanging around, trying to peek into the windows, and the guards ordered them away.

'Get out your press card,' Amy told her, and Tasha did. Together they approached the man who was standing guard in front of the door.

'What should I ask him?' Tasha whispered in a panic.

Amy recalled watching a reporter on the TV news. 'Don't ask, just show him the press card and tell him you need to see whoever is in charge.'

Tasha's hand trembled as she held up the card. She started to speak, but her voice squeaked. 'I – I need to say, I mean I need to see—'

The guard wasn't even paying attention to her. He was looking directly at Amy. 'I see you've got a new hairstyle,' he said with a smile. 'Very nice. Is this your friend?' He opened the door of the mobile home and ushered them in.

4

Amy had never been inside a mobile home before, but she suspected that ordinary mobile homes didn't look anything like this one. The vehicle she and Tasha entered looked like the kind of room you'd expect to find in a luxury resort hotel. It was all white and yellow and green, with pale wood furniture covered in soft, light green cushions. Gauzy curtains floated over the windows. The wallpaper was printed with yellow roses, and there were real yellow roses in white ceramic vases on every surface. Small potted palm trees were positioned around the room, and the general atmosphere made it feel like they were walking into a garden.

Along one wall was an elaborate electronic system, which included a TV, VCR, stereo, computer, fax machine, and telephone. All the equipment was pale yellow, to blend in with the general colour scheme.

Only the sound of angry voices disturbed the tranquil environment.

'What's your problem?' A male voice came from behind a curtain that divided this room from the rest of the trailer.

The young, female voice that responded was vaguely familiar. 'I don't want to *be* here.'

'You don't want to be in the movie?'

'That's not what I said. I just don't feel like traipsing around this crummy school.'

'Well, this crummy school just happens to be the setting for the movie I am about to direct. We're going to be filming a lot of scenes here, and you need to familiarise yourself with the place. I want you to get the feel of it, absorb the ambiance—'

'I'm the star of this movie!' the girl yelled. 'Get someone else to absorb the stupid ambiance.'

Tasha didn't need any kind of super-hearing to pick up on this. 'I don't think Parkside's *that* crummy,' she whispered.

'Shhh!' Amy hissed. The two girls jumped back

against the wall as the curtain was pushed aside and a grey-haired man stormed out. He didn't even see Amy and Tasha as he strode out of the trailer, slamming the door behind him.

'Yikes!' Tasha whispered.

'Maybe this isn't the best day to talk to the director,' Amy murmured. She glanced at the curtain. 'Or the star.'

Tasha agreed. 'Let's get out of here.'

Amy thought they were both speaking softly, but the girl must have heard them. 'Is someone there?' she called out sharply. 'Who's in my trailer?'

Amy grabbed Tasha's hand, but they couldn't move fast enough. Once again the curtain was brushed aside, and a girl appeared in the room.

Amy gasped. The world came to an abrupt halt. The universe went still, the earth stopped spinning. She was frozen in place, unable to move, unable to breathe.

The other girl, too, appeared stunned. Her eyes widened. She was Amy's height, and Amy's shape. She wore a yellow satin robe, tied at the waist. Her hair was blonde, and it hung down her back in spiral curls.

But in every other way, Amy could have been

looking at her own reflection. The eyes, the mouth, the nose . . . each feature of the girl's face was exactly like Amy's.

Amy's head began to spin, and she thought she might faint. She saw the same shock of recognition in the other girl's eyes. Tasha saw it, too. Amy felt Tasha's hand tightening on her own, and from somewhere far away she heard Tasha saying, 'Oh-migosh,' in a voice that was barely audible.

Amy didn't know how long they stood there, staring at each other. It seemed like an eternity, but it could only have been a few seconds.

Finally Amy spoke, and she said the only thing that came to her mind.

'Amy?'

The other girl opened her mouth, but no words came out. Instead, there was a noise . . . a low moan that grew louder and escalated into a shriek.

The door burst open and the burly guard who had admitted them to the trailer ran in. 'What's going on?'

'Get them out of here! Now!' the actress screamed at him.

The man looked at Amy and then at the actress. For a moment he seemed totally confused, his eyes darting back and forth between them in disbelief. 'What the – I thought—'

But as the actress continued to scream at him, he went into action. Roughly he grabbed Amy's arm with one hand and Tasha's arm with the other. The girls put up no resistance as he pulled them out of the trailer and yelled at them to beat it.

Then Tasha took over. Still holding Amy's hand, she dragged her away from the school grounds. For once, it was Tasha who was moving faster and in the lead. Amy stumbled along, barely able to put one foot in front of the other. Barely able to see, or hear . . . and totally unable to think.

As for speech, all she could do was repeat the same words over and over again.

'That was Amy. Another Amy.'

5

'**Y**our colour's coming back,' Tasha said as
she handed Amy her third glass of water in
less than five minutes.

Amy could feel her breath coming easier too,
although her heart was still pounding harder and
faster than usual. She drank the water in one gulp,
then sank back onto the pillows Tasha had propped
up on her bed.

'How are you feeling now?' Tasha asked anxiously.

'I'm okay.'

'I thought you were going to pass out back there.'

'Can you blame me?' Amy asked.

'No. It was a pretty freaky experience.'

Amy nodded.

'I guess that was why the guard let us in so easily,' Tasha mused. 'He thought you were her, with different hair.'

Again Amy could only bob her head up and down in agreement.

'Of course,' Tasha continued, 'it's not like this was the first time you've had this happen to you.'

Amy knew that Tasha was referring to the French dancer. At that time, Amy had been totally floored by the coincidence of finding herself in the same general vicinity, under the same roof, as another Amy. And now, today, she had come face-to-face with one.

She was very glad Tasha had been there to witness the encounter. 'It wasn't my imagination, was it?' she asked Tasha. She didn't really doubt herself, but she wanted confirmation.

Tasha gave it to her. 'It wasn't your imagination. That actress was your twin.' After a moment she said, 'I guess *twin* really isn't the right word. What would you call her? Your replica?'

It was a creepy word, Amy thought. Artificial and not quite human. There had to be something else she could call the actress.

'I've seen her before,' Tasha declared.

'You have?' Amy asked in astonishment. 'Why didn't you tell me?'

'I *did* tell you, remember? I saw her on that TV commercial.'

Amy decided that from now on she would trust Tasha's observations. But it was so hard to believe. 'There are twelve Amys in the world,' she said, 'and two of them have turned up in Los Angeles in the space of a month. Three, including me. What are the odds of that happening?'

'I haven't the slightest idea,' Tasha said. 'And how do you know for sure there are only twelve Amys?'

'My mother was working in the lab, remember? And she can count.'

Tasha persisted. 'But she wouldn't necessarily know if there were other experiments going on, in other laboratories, with the exact same genes and DNA stuff. There could be hundreds of Amys, thousands of Amys . . .'

'Tasha,' Amy moaned, 'you're giving me a head-ache.'

'Sorry,' Tasha said automatically. Then she grinned. 'You liar. You've never had a headache in your life.'

'Well, if I *could* have a headache, I'd be having one now.'

Tasha sat down on the edge of the bed. 'What does it feel like?' she asked. 'Knowing there are others exactly like you?'

'I'm not sure what I feel,' Amy confessed. 'When I first knew what I was, I thought it would be creepy to meet another clone. But when we went to the ballet and I saw that dancer, I wanted to meet her and talk to her. Know her.'

'Is that how you feel about the actress?'

Amy nodded. 'Seeing her up close – close enough to touch . . . it was, I don't know, scary and thrilling, at the same time.'

'There's something I wonder about, though,' Tasha remarked. 'She didn't *sound* like you. I mean, her voice was the same, but the way she was yelling and whining. I can't imagine you carrying on like that.'

'She was just in a bad mood,' Amy said. 'Even clones have moods, you know. You've heard me yell. And I can definitely whine.'

'I wonder what her name is,' Tasha mused.

'We'll know tomorrow,' Amy declared. 'We're going back to that trailer.'

'We are?'

'Well, *I* am, and you can come too, if you want.'

Tasha grimaced. 'Are you sure that's such a good idea? She wasn't exactly thrilled to see you.'

Amy brushed that aside. 'Hey, she was freaked out; you can't blame her for that. I was blown away too. Once she calms down, she'll want to see me again.' She jumped off the bed as a wave of excitement rushed through her. 'Oh, Tasha, there will be so much we can talk about! Experiences and feelings to compare . . . I mean, you're my best friend in all the world, and I could never be closer to anyone else, but the idea of finding someone who knows exactly what I am . . .'

'I understand,' Tasha assured her. 'Don't worry, I'm not going to be jealous.'

They heard a door open downstairs, and then a voice called, 'Amy?'

'I'm up here, Mom.'

A moment later Nancy Candler came into the bedroom. 'Hi, Tasha. Amy – what's wrong?'

'What makes you think something's wrong?' Amy asked innocently.

'I know my daughter, that's what,' her mother

said dryly. 'And there isn't an expression you can come up with that I wouldn't recognise.'

Amy laughed. 'Well, nothing's wrong. In fact . . . something's very right.'

'What's that?'

'I think I'd better go now,' Tasha announced. 'You two will want to have a mother-daughter conversation, talk about this privately. I'll call you later, Amy.'

Nancy looked at Tasha's departing figure with suspicion and curiosity, which she then directed towards Amy. 'Okay, what's up?'

Amy wasn't sure how to begin. 'Mom, there's something I never told you.'

Apprehension crossed Nancy's face. She sat down on Amy's bed and put a hand over her heart, as if she was preparing herself for the worst.

'Nothing terrible,' Amy assured her quickly. She sat down next to her. 'It's something that happened while you were in the hospital. I didn't want to tell you about it then. Well, actually, I *couldn't*. I mean, you were in a coma. And then, afterwards, you weren't exactly in a great mood.'

'Amy, get to the point.'

'Well, it was when Mrs Morgan took us to see

The Nutcracker. There was a dancer in the ballet. She looked exactly like me.'

Nancy didn't say anything.

'I looked for her after the programme,' Amy went on. 'But she'd already left.'

'And you saw her again today?' her mother asked.

'No. I found another one.' Amy told her mother the whole story, about going to the mobile home and encountering the star of the movie. 'She's another one like me, Mom. Another Amy.'

Her mother was quiet for a minute. 'Amy, sweetie, you can't be sure about this. The girl you saw in the ballet, the girl you saw today – it's very possible that they are both just two ordinary girls who bear a resemblance to you. You know, they say everyone in the world has a twin some-where.'

'And some of us have triplets?' Amy shook her head. 'I don't think so, Mom.'

At least Nancy was taking her seriously. 'How did the other girl react when she saw you today?'

'She flipped,' Amy replied. 'I guess that's natural; I was shook up too. To run into your own clone like that—'

Nancy broke in. 'She may not even have realised what was happening.'

'Huh?'

'Amy, even if this girl *is* your clone, it's conceivable that she has no knowledge of what she is. Maybe no one ever told her. It's possible that her parents don't even know her background. This information wasn't included when the infants were sent to orphanages.'

'But she has to know she's different from other people. *I* did.'

'That's because you were in situations that made your unique qualities and talents apparent. You were taking gymnastics, and suddenly you found you could do all the routines better than anyone else. You went to an ice-skating party never having ice-skated in your life, and you performed like an Olympic champion. Maybe this girl has never been in a similar situation.'

'But it was more than that,' Amy protested. 'I knew I could hear and see better than other people, I could run faster, I could throw a ball farther . . .'

'You knew because you had other people around to compare yourself to,' Nancy said. 'You had friends who pointed your skills out to you. Maybe

54

this girl you saw today hasn't been as social as you are. Maybe she thinks she's ordinary, that everyone in the world sees and hears like she does.'

'She'd have to have been awfully sheltered,' Amy objected. 'Like, locked up in solitary confinement or something.'

Her mother considered this. 'You said she's an actress, right? She could have a stage mother, who—'

'A what?' Amy interrupted.

'A mother who hovers over her child, watches her all the time, worries about her constantly.'

Amy grinned mischievously. 'Oh yeah, I once knew a mother like that.'

'I was never that bad with you,' Nancy protested. 'And a stage mother is different. She wants her child to be a big success in show business; she's constantly on the lookout for competition. She's overprotective, and she keeps her child away from others her own age. I'm serious, Amy. This girl could have no idea that she's any different from anyone else.'

'Mom, come on—'

'And like I said before, she could be someone who just looks like you and that's all. Nothing more.'

Amy got up and went to the mirror. She gazed at her reflection, concentrating on her hair. She imagined it blonde and curly.

Her mother was wrong. No two people could look that much alike without being related. That actress shared something very basic with Amy. Something that went far beyond chance and coincidence.

'She's just like me, Mom. She's a clone. And if she doesn't know that already, she should.'

'Amy, please. Stay away from her.'

'I can't! I want to know her. She'll want to know me.'

'You can't be sure of that,' Nancy argued. 'That girl could be perfectly happy and contented just as she is.' She let out a sigh. 'You know, as a teacher, I never thought I would say this. But sometimes ignorance *is* bliss.'

Amy countered this with another classic saying. 'And the truth will set you free.'

'Amy . . .'

'Mom, she's like me. She could be in danger, like me. She needs to be warned – she has to stay alert. She can't protect herself unless she knows everything about herself. She has a right to know the truth.'

'She doesn't need to learn it from you,' Nancy pointed out.

'Then who is she going to learn it from?'

Nancy fell silent. Amy returned to the bed and sat down. Nancy put an arm around her. Finally she spoke.

'I can't forbid you to seek out this girl, Amy. But do me – and her, and yourself – a favour. Go easy on her. Be very, very careful. Keep in mind what a shock it was to you when you found out who you really are. If, and I repeat, *if*, this girl is a clone and doesn't know it, the revelation could be traumatic.'

'I'll be careful,' Amy assured her. 'I'll understand how she feels. We're identical, Mom, remember?'

'But even if it's true, if she is another Amy, remember that you're only identical in a genetic sense.'

'Isn't that everything?'

'Not at all. You may have been born with identical genetic structure, but since then you've had different upbringings. The way someone is nurtured, the values she learns, the experiences she has – these help to make a person what she is. Science has shown us that identical twins who are separated at birth may end up having a lot in common, but their personalities can be totally different. This girl, this actress – she may not be the kind of person you think she is.'

Amy considered this. 'I won't know until I know her, will I?' She leaned over to get another glimpse of herself in the mirror. Nancy put her hand under Amy's chin and gently drew her face to meet her own.

'Just be careful, Amy. You don't know what you're getting yourself into here.'

Amy didn't want to be rude, but she couldn't resist saying, 'Neither do you.'

'That's true,' Nancy said. 'And I know I'll never be able to completely understand what you feel. I've learned that I have to let you live your own life.' She leaned forward and kissed Amy's forehead. 'Just always remember that I love you. You may not be the child of my body, but you're the child of my heart. And I don't want to see you get hurt, in any possible way.'

Amy hugged her mother. 'It's okay, Mom. I can deal with this.' She spoke with a confidence that she really felt.

Nancy didn't look anywhere near as confident.

But Amy couldn't expect her to. After all, Nancy hadn't just come face-to-face with—

Suddenly Amy knew what to call the actress. Not a clone, a twin, or a replica.

A sister.

6

A my had warned Tasha by phone that she wanted to get to school a half hour earlier than usual the next morning. It was only in the past few months that Tasha had gotten into the habit of showing up at Amy's door on time. Amy wasn't holding much hope that Tasha would come by for her early.

But once again, she underestimated her best friend. Precisely thirty minutes before their usual departure time, Tasha was on the doorstep. When Amy opened the door to her, Tasha yawned in her face.

'Don't expect me to be too upbeat,' she grumbled. 'I've had thirty minutes less sleep than I'm used to. I hope you appreciate the sacrifice.'

'I do, I do,' Amy said, feeling upbeat enough for the two of them. 'Mom! Tasha's here, I'm leaving!'

'Have a nice day, girls,' Nancy called from upstairs. 'And Amy, *please*, remember what I said.'

'I'll remember,' Amy called back. She hurried out the door before her mother could remind her again.

'Remember what?' Tasha asked.

'Mom doesn't want me to pounce on the actress,' Amy said cheerfully. 'She says I should take it easy when I talk to her, because she might not know anything about herself. It could be a real trauma for her when she finds out.'

'And you're going to tell her?' Tasha asked in alarm. 'No offence, Amy, since she may be your clone, but after seeing the way she behaved yesterday, I wouldn't want to be giving her any news she doesn't want to hear.'

'Give me some credit,' Amy said. 'I'm not going to throw my arms around her and yell, 'Hey, sister!' I'll have to win her trust first and make friends with her.'

'How do you plan on doing that?'

'First I'll go by the trailer and apologise for bursting in on her yesterday.'

Tasha was sceptical. 'I hope you get a chance to say something before she starts screaming again.'

'She won't scream,' Amy said with confidence. 'She's had time to recover from the shock and get used to the idea that someone looks like her. She'll be curious, and she'll *want* to talk to me.'

'And while you two are having your heart-to-heart, clone-to-clone conversation, what am I supposed to be doing? Just sticking around in case she goes on the offensive and you need help fighting her off?'

'Don't be silly,' Amy scolded her. 'Once she becomes my friend, she'll be your friend too.'

'Goody, goody,' Tasha commented.

'Don't be sarcastic. Tasha, think about it, this could be great for you. If you guys become friends, you'll be able to get all the inside dope about the movie. She'll introduce you to all the important people, maybe even arrange for you to watch some of the filming. You'll write a brilliant article for the *Journal* and become a famous reporter!'

'Yeah, I guess that could happen,' Tasha said thoughtfully.

'Of course, if the conversation between me and the actress gets really intense and we start talking about stuff you wouldn't understand—'

'Don't worry, I'll know when my presence is no longer desired.'

Amy smiled at her friend gratefully. Then she glanced over her shoulder.

'If you're looking for Eric, forget it,' Tasha told her. 'There's no way he'd get out of bed thirty minutes early.'

'Did you tell him about the actress?'

'No, the only time I saw him was at the dinner table, and I couldn't bring it up in front of my parents.'

'Did he say anything about yesterday?' Amy pressed. 'Is he still mad at me?'

'I don't know! Like I said, I didn't talk to him. For crying out loud, stop worrying, it's only Eric.'

He might have been 'only Eric' to Tasha, but Amy saw him from a different perspective. Tasha just didn't get it. Amy wasn't going to fret about Eric now, though. She was too excited, and she couldn't wait to get to school.

'Slow down!' Tasha exclaimed. 'Some of us are just ordinary human beings, you know. Hey, have you thought about what's going to happen when other kids at Parkside see the actress? They're bound to notice how much you two look alike. What are you going to say?'

'First of all, I'll bet some of them won't even see a resemblance,' Amy replied. 'Hair colour can make a big difference in a person's appearance. And if they do notice, well, I'll just say that everyone is supposed to have a twin somewhere.'

They weren't the first people to arrive at school. The teachers were already there, and so were students who'd come to use the library before homeroom. Still, there were no kids hanging out in front of the building. And the mobile home was in the same place it had been the day before.

Amy and Tasha approached it with trepidation. If the same guard was on duty, they were going to have a rough time convincing him to let them see the actress.

But he wasn't there. There were no guards at all in front of the mobile home. Amy was amazed at her luck. This was almost too good to be true. She adjusted her headband and tried to tuck her T-shirt into her jeans more neatly.

'How do I look?' she asked anxiously.

Tasha rolled her eyes. Amy laughed nervously and knocked on the mobile home's door.

No answer. Amy knocked again. Then she pressed her ear against the door.

'Hear anything?' Tasha asked.

Amy shook her head. 'No one's in there. Where could she be so early?'

'Amy, I don't think she actually *lives* in that trailer. I went on a Hollywood studio tour once, and there were trailers like this all over the place. Our guide said the actors hang out in them while they're waiting to be called onto the set.'

'Oh, well, I'm glad I didn't wake her up,' Amy said. 'That could definitely get things off on the wrong foot. She'll show up eventually. I just hope it's before the bell.'

'Something's going on,' Tasha said. 'Look, they're bringing equipment into the gym entrance. Ooh, I hope that means we won't have phys ed today.'

Amy watched as men in jeans dragged huge cameras and lights into the building. Then her gaze was drawn to a small plate next to the mobile home's door. 'Tasha, look!'

A name was spelled out in gold letters. 'Aimee Evans,' Tasha read, pronouncing it 'Aye-may.'

'No, I'm sure it's pronounced 'Amy,' it's just spelled in a fancy way,' Amy said. 'Oh, Tasha, she *is* my clone, she has to be! This couldn't be a coincidence!'

Tasha looked at her watch. 'It's only ten minutes till the bell.'

They didn't have to wait that long. A car pulled up in front of the school, and two men jumped out. One of them was the guard from yesterday, and when he saw the girls in front of the mobile home, he wasn't pleased.

'What are you two doing here?' he demanded.

'I have to talk to Aimee Evans,' Amy told him.

'Forget it,' he barked. 'Get out of here.'

'Please,' she begged, 'it's important.'

He shook his head. 'Sorry, kid. Just because you look like her doesn't mean you're going to be her best friend.'

'No kidding,' Tasha said stoutly.

He ignored her. 'Look, don't make trouble, okay? Aimee Evans doesn't want to see you.'

'How can you be so sure?'

'Because I was here yesterday!'

'She could have changed her mind.'

'Franklin, what's going on over here?' The grey-haired man they'd seen previously was coming towards them. When he saw Amy, he gasped in

horror. 'What did you do to your hair?' he practically shrieked.

'Take it easy, Mr Hardy,' the guard said. 'This
isn't Aimee Evans. She's some kid from the school
who looks like her.'

Mr Hardy was clearly relieved, but he was still
frowning. 'Aimee isn't going to like that.'

'She doesn't like it already,' Franklin told him.
'These girls were here yesterday, and Aimee threw a
fit.'

'What else is new?' Mr Hardy muttered. He
turned to look at the school. 'Students have to
be kept out of the way. I'm going to talk to the
principal right now.' He started in that direction.

Tasha ran after him. 'Mr Hardy, wait, I'm a
reporter. I have a press card – look,' she called as
she tried to open her bag. The contents poured out
onto the cement. Mr Hardy didn't even look back.

Amy helped her gather her stuff, and the guard
helped too, but he wasn't any more cordial than
he'd been before. 'I don't want to see either of you
kids around here again, do you hear me?'

'Oh, this is great, just great,' Tasha moaned. 'I
won't be able to write about the movie, and now
we're going to be reported to the principal.'

'Don't worry, he doesn't know our names,' Amy said. Her thoughts were in a jumble. This wasn't turning out as she had planned. She was going to have to come up with another way to make contact with Aimee.

The girls separated to go to their homerooms. Amy found her homeroom class in a state of excitement – half a dozen girls were gathered around Jeanine, giggling like hyenas.

Linda Riviera was semi-hysterical. 'Jeanine, are you serious? Is this for real? We're going to be in the movie?'

'*Maybe*,' Jeanine said. 'You have to be chosen. And it won't be a real part, of course. They just need extras.'

'Extra what?' Amy asked, joining the group. She knew she was doing exactly what Jeanine wanted her to do, acknowledging that the girl had information Amy didn't. Still, she was curious enough to give her rival a thrill.

'The director is looking for people to be in the background for some scenes,' Jeanine informed her importantly. 'They want kids who look like ordinary students.'

'So we'll be perfect,' Linda said.

'Some of you will be perfect,' Jeanine corrected her. Her eyes swept over Amy. 'I'm sure they only want kids who look halfway decent.'

Amy tried not to smile. Apparently, Jeanine had not yet seen the star. 'Don't worry, Jeanine, I'm not going to compete with you. I have no desire to be an extra.'

'Oh, *I'm* not going to be an extra,' Jeanine declared. 'I'll have a real part, with a name.' She turned to the others. 'If you want to be extras, you're supposed to show up after school in the gym. The director's going to pick the people he wants.'

The bell rang, the teacher came in, and kids raced to their seats. Amy sat down and digested this latest titbit of information. So some kids *would* be able to get onto the film set, and maybe close to Aimee. But there was no point in her going to the gym for the tryouts. Or Tasha either, for that matter. Amy sincerely doubted that Mr Hardy would give them a chance. In fact, he'd probably order Franklin to throw both of them out of the gym.

But Jeanine's news had given her an idea.

She couldn't find Tasha until lunchtime, when they met in the cafeteria as usual. Amy reported what she'd learned in homeroom.

'There's no way we're getting parts as extras,' Tasha pointed out.

'I know, I know,' Amy said. 'But I was thinking about Eric.'

'Eric! You have to be kidding. He'd never get cast.'

Amy shook her head. 'He's the only one who can help me. He'll understand why I have to talk to Aimee, and Mr Hardy's never seen him, so at least he's got a chance of being picked. Then he could talk to Aimee, and arrange for us to get together, and—'

'Aren't you forgetting something?' Tasha asked. 'What if Eric doesn't *want* to be an extra? He doesn't even like having his picture taken, Amy. I don't think he'll be too crazy about the idea of being in a movie.'

Amy chewed on a fingernail and considered this possibility.

Tasha watched her with interest. 'There's something I've always meant to ask you. When you bite your fingernails off, do they grow back overnight?'

'I never noticed,' Amy said impatiently. 'Listen, Tasha, this is important. We have to talk Eric into doing this.'

'*We?*' Tasha asked. 'Maybe you haven't noticed, but I've never been able to talk my brother into anything.'

'And he's mad at me,' Amy moaned. 'What am I going to do?'

'Have you considered bribery?'

Tasha was joking, but Amy knew she'd hit on the answer.

Once again, she positioned herself just outside the cafeteria, where she could attract Eric's attention without embarrassing him in front of his friends. When the students poured out, she moved swiftly so no one would notice, and gave Eric's shirt a tug. He turned, saw her, and frowned. She put her hands together as if in prayer and looked at him pleadingly. Curiosity overcame his annoyance.

'What's up?'

'First of all, I want to tell you again how very, very sorry I am about yesterday.'

'Yeah, okay. Is that all?'

Amy took a deep breath, and her words came out in a rush. 'They're looking for kids to be extras in the movie and if you go to the gym after school today you can try out.'

'Are you nuts?' He turned to walk away, but

Amy grabbed his arm *hard*. He wasn't going anywhere.

'What are you doing?' He winced. 'Let go of
me!'

'Just listen to me, okay?' She spoke in a whisper.

'The girl who's the star of the movie, I think she's
a – well, I think she's like me, if you know what I
mean.'

His eyebrows shot up. 'You think she's a cl—'

'Shhh!' Then Amy nodded. 'I've been trying to
talk to her, but I can't get near her. The director's
seen me, and Tasha, too, so he won't pick either of
us to be an extra. Eric, please, you have to do this
for me! I have to make contact with her!'

Eric was distinctly uncomfortable with the request. 'No way, Amy. I don't want to be an actor.'

'You don't have to be an actor,' Amy said. 'You
probably won't have to do anything more than stand
still, or walk, or sit. Come on, Eric . . .' She could see
he wasn't convinced. It was time to offer the bribe.

'Remember Ronald Hurley?' she asked.

'What about him?'

'You wanted me to spy on him and find out what
level of Disaster Isle he's at. If you go to the gym this
afternoon and try out, I'll do it.'

She detected a spark of interest on his face. 'What if I don't get picked as an extra? Will you still spy on him?'

Amy nodded.

Eric considered the deal. Then his eyes lit up. 'Hey, I've got this huge maths assignment due next week. You could probably whip it out in five minutes. Do that for me, and I'll go to the gym for you.'

Amy winced. A little harmless spying was one thing. Doing someone else's homework was something else. 'I can't, Eric,' she said regretfully. 'It's not right.'

Eric bit his lip. 'But you'll definitely find out what level Hurley's on? Today?'

Amy nodded. 'As soon as I get home from school, I'll go straight to his house and wait by the window. If he plays on his computer, I'll see what he does and tell you tonight. Deal?'

She held her breath.

Eric frowned and scratched his head with his free hand. 'Will you let go of my arm now?'

She nodded.

'Deal.'

7

E ric felt unbelievably weird. He slipped into the gym as unobtrusively as possible and pressed himself against the wall, at the back of the bleachers, where he was least likely to be noticed by any of the others milling around.

What was he *doing* here? No one else in his crowd, none of his buddies, was volunteering to be an extra. From his vantage point, he surveyed the people who *were* and decided that each fell into one of three categories: girls from grades seven to nine; boys from grades seven and eight; nerdy boys from grade nine. So where did he fit in?

He was overwhelmed with a sense of being somewhere he absolutely did not want to be. He could make a fast escape right now, he thought. As far as he could tell, no one had seen him come in. Was it really worth the possibility of being considered a ninth-grade nerd? Did he really need to know if Ronald Hurley was lying about his level in Disaster Isle?

But Amy would be really mad if he didn't go through with this. Not that he owed her anything after the way she'd treated him the day before. Still, she was acting like she was honestly sorry. And he could understand why she'd get uptight about people keeping secrets. Plus, he had to admit, he was kind of curious about seeing another clone.

But on the other hand, should he risk his reputation as a fairly cool guy?

Right now he didn't see anyone in the gym who looked like Amy. But if this other clone was the star of the movie, he imagined she wouldn't be hanging out with wannabe extras.

A shrill whistle, like the one his basketball coach used, pierced the air. This was followed by a woman's voice speaking into a microphone. 'Boys, please line up on the right side of the gym. Girls, line up on the left side.'

It was decision time. Amy's face popped into Eric's head. He walked over to the right side of the gym.

Unfortunately, it turned out that the woman was talking about the right side as perceived from her end of the gym, not his. He found himself joining a line of giggling girls. With his face already flushed, he hurried over to the other side and got into line, just behind a major dork from his biology class, a guy named Nick, who always reminded him of one of the animals they dissected. Eric wanted to die.

Each of them was handed a large index card with a number on it. Eric's number was twelve. They were instructed to turn, face forward, and hold the cards up in front of their chests.

As this was happening, Eric checked out the girls facing him on the other side of the gym. He recognised Jeanine, who took gymnastics with his sister, and who was always flipping her hair over her shoulder. He hoped they wouldn't be extras together. She made him nervous.

Now a woman with dark hair and a lot of make-up was conferring with a grey-haired man. They split up, and the man walked slowly down the row of girls. The woman walked in front of the boys, scrutinising each one. Suddenly Eric thought he knew how a piece of beef must feel when his mother was choosing meat from the butcher's counter in the supermarket. He hadn't felt this exposed since taking his physical for the basketball team. At least he was fully clothed here.

When the woman finished perusing them, he had no idea what to expect next. What if they were asked to dance? Or sing? Well, if that was the case, Amy could just forget it – he was out of here.

The woman came back down the line. He could feel his face getting redder by the minute. In two seconds he was going to bolt.

The woman and the man conferred again. Then the woman spoke into the microphone. 'If we call out your number, please take a seat on the bleachers. The rest of you may leave. Two, five, eleven, twelve . . .'

Twelve – that was him! Eric was surprised. Was that it? All they cared about was how the students looked? He was actually a little flattered – until he realised that number eleven was Nick, the toad from biology. He wanted to die again.

He took a seat as far from Nick as possible. But then Jeanine came over and sat down next to him. He didn't know which was worse.

'Eric!' she exclaimed. 'I didn't know you were interested in acting!'

He shifted uncomfortably in his seat. 'Do extras have to act?'

'I don't know. *I'm* not an extra,' Jeanine bragged. 'I have a real part. With a name.'

'What kind of a part?'

Jeanine giggled. 'I don't know. I guess I'll find out pretty soon. Ooh, Eric, maybe you could help me memorise my lines!'

He looked at her in horror. But now the man was standing in front of the bleachers, calling for their attention.

'Good afternoon. My name is Mr Hardy, and I am the director of *Middle School Maniac*. All twenty-five of you have been selected to be extras in this film, because together you represent a realistic-looking class of middle school students.'

Eric suddenly felt better about being in the same group as Nick. After all, every school had to have its share of nerds.

'How many of you have any film experience?' the director asked.

'Do home movies count?' someone yelled.

'No.' Mr Hardy gazed over the group. 'Fine. Now, let me tell you what you'll be doing.'

As Eric listened to Mr Hardy describe the job of

being an extra, his spirits began to rise. They wouldn't have to memorise any lines. They'd actually be excused from some classes to participate in the filming! And the best news of all – they would be paid! Not a fortune, but enough to buy Disaster Isle 2.

'And now,' Mr Hardy continued, 'let me tell you about *Middle School Maniac*. This is the first production in what is anticipated to be an ongoing series about a psychotic killer who stalks middle school students. When the killer was in middle school, he was beaten up and ridiculed by other kids for his unattractive appearance. He vowed to take revenge on them when he grew up. He becomes a substitute teacher and goes from middle school to middle school, where he maims or kills every kid who reminds him of his old classmates.'

A hand went up. It was Nerdy Nick. 'Why doesn't he just go after the people who really hurt him?'

Mr Hardy clearly hadn't expected any questions. 'Because . . . because he's a *psychotic* killer,' he replied. 'Everyone thinks the murders are being committed by another student, Marco, who was recently released from a mental institution. He was committed there after killing his evil twin brother, who had planned to destroy the world. So this boy actually did everyone a favour, but they don't know that. And now I would like to introduce the actor who will be playing that student.' He paused dramatically, then yelled out, 'Rory Keller!'

Squeals went up from some of the girls. 'Who's Rory Keller?' Eric asked Jeanine.

'He was on a soap opera, *Malibu Secrets*,' she told him excitedly. She was applauding wildly as the boy came into the gym.

Eric had never watched *Malibu Secrets* – or even heard of it – so the boy who stood before them was a total stranger. But Eric had to admit, Rory Keller looked like someone who would kill his own brother. He had black hair, piercing black eyes, thin lips, and a surly expression. And he was scrawny. While the girls continued to squeal and applaud, Eric tried to understand what they would see in a guy like that. He figured it was just another female mystery.

Rory took a bow. Mr Hardy went on with the story of *Middle School Maniac*.

'But there's one person who doesn't believe that Rory – or Marco, I should say – is responsible for the middle-school murders. She's committed to finding the real killer. In the role of Amanda, a young lady you may not know, but who is destined to become a great star. Aimee Evans!'

The applause was not quite as enthusiastic for the unknown actress, but Eric watched her come into the gym with real interest. She *did* look like Amy, except that she was blonde and looked older, but that was probably the make-up. She was kind of pretty, in a dressed-up way. She didn't look any more like a clone than Amy did – but then he didn't know what a clone should look like, anyway.

Aimee smiled brightly and took her bow. Then she joined the other movie people at a long table.

Mr Hardy continued, 'If any of you kids have weak stomachs, I'd better warn you right now, you're going to see some pretty gory stuff. There will be the usual stabbings, drownings, and strangulations, plus some dismemberment and general mutilation. And, of course, buckets of blood. Anyone have a problem with this?'

No one expressed any concern. 'Sounds good to me,' whispered someone sitting behind Eric. Jeanine wrinkled her nose and made a noise that sounded like 'eeew,' but she didn't speak out.

Mr Hardy was satisfied. 'Okay, we're cool, we're happening. My production assistant will hand out contracts. Take them home, get them signed by a parent, bring them back here tomorrow morning at eight o'clock.'

Eric's stomach plunged. Eight o'clock – a full half hour before he normally had to be at school! Amy had better appreciate this. And then, of course, there was the money . . .

The forms were distributed and the kids were excused. Now it was time for Eric to make his first contact with the actress. He had absolutely no idea what he was going to say to her. He just hoped something would come to him.

But as he approached the long table he saw that he wasn't the only one who wanted to meet Aimee Evans. Jeanine had already cornered her. Eric ambled over anyway.

'I'm so excited to be in this movie,' he heard Jeanine say. 'But I still don't know what role I'm playing! I was going to talk to Mr Hardy now, but then I thought maybe I'd talk to you first. Because you'd be more sympathetic.'

In Eric's opinion, Aimee Evans didn't look particularly sympathetic, but Jeanine continued. 'You see, I'm supposed to be more than an extra, and I'm sure Mr Hardy knows that. This could be my big chance to break into the movie business, so I want a really good part. Anyway, I was wondering if you could put in a word for me.'

Aimee smiled. 'Sure. No problem.'

'Really? That's so sweet of you! I really, really appreciate this, Aimee. I just know we're going to be great friends.' And Jeanine skipped off.

Aimee stared after her. The smile disappeared. She spoke in a low voice, but loudly enough for Eric to hear. 'In your dreams.'

Eric was startled. Okay, Jeanine was a stuck-up pain, but Aimee couldn't know that, not yet. Or maybe she could. He tried to remember whether Amy had ever said anything about clones being hypersensitive to personalities.

Or maybe he'd just heard wrong. After all, *he* didn't have any superpowers.

He was about to approach the actress, but a short, plump woman got to her first. 'Aimee, I need for you to try on the long dress for the formal dance scene.'

'Now?'

'Yes, now.'

Aimee pouted. 'I don't feel like trying on clothes now.'

The woman's lips tightened, as if she'd heard this before. 'Well, I'm sorry about that, Aimee, but you're going to be shooting that scene in just a few days, and I need to make some alterations in the dress.'

'I'll do it tomorrow,' Aimee said.

'I don't have the time to fit you tomorrow.'

Aimee's eyes narrowed. '*Make* the time.'

The woman was distinctly annoyed. 'Aimee, your attitude is completely unprofessional. I don't want to speak to Mr Hardy about you, but'—'

'No, I don't think that's a good idea,' Aimee interrupted. 'Because then I'd have to speak to Mr Hardy about *you*.'

'What are you talking about?'

Aimee smiled, but it wasn't a pretty smile. 'I've seen you picking up those scraps of fabric in the costume department. And I know what you've been doing with them.'

The woman stared at her in disbelief.

'I followed you to your office,' Aimee said. 'Did you know there's a fire hydrant just outside your window? It was easy for me to stand on it and see you.' She paused. Her smiled broadened and looked even meaner. 'You were sewing those scraps together, making a quilt. And I can guess what you do with those quilts. You sell them.'

The woman protested, 'Aimee, those scraps are leftover material. They would just go into the garbage.'

'The *studio's* garbage,' Aimee said. 'You were taking stuff that didn't belong to you. You're making money from studio property. I believe that constitutes theft.'

'Mr Hardy wouldn't care if I kept fabric scraps!'

'No? Why don't we just ask him right now and find out.'

The director was heading their way. He was rubbing his hands together, and he looked pleased with himself. 'That went well, I think. What's your problem, Sylvia?'

The costume woman didn't say anything. Aimee spoke. 'There's no problem, Mr Hardy. Everything's fine. Sylvia and I were just talking about my next fitting. We're doing it tomorrow. Aren't we, Sylvia?'

Sylvia looked at Aimee long and hard. But all she said was 'Yes,' before walking away.

Eric coughed. 'Uh, hi, I'm—'

But Aimee hadn't finished talking to Mr Hardy. 'I want to tell you about one of the extras. Jeanine Something.'

Mr Hardy picked up a list from the table. 'Jeanine, Jeanine . . . oh yes, here she is. What about her?'

'Get rid of her.'

'What?'

'You heard me. Get rid of her. I don't like her looks.'

Mr Hardy's face took on the same expression Eric had seen on the wardrobe woman. 'You're not running this show, Aimee.'

'It's her or me,' Aimee said. 'If I quit now, how far behind schedule will that put you?'

Mr Hardy looked pained. He examined the list again. 'Wait a minute, there's a note here about her. Her father's president of the bank that's making a major investment in the film. The producer promised him Jeanine would have a role.'

Aimee was momentarily stumped. Then she smiled that awful smile again. 'All right. She can play Marcia.' From her satisfied expression, Eric concluded that Marcia wasn't a very desirable role.

Aimee then turned away and started out of the gym. Eric followed her. 'Uh, excuse me, Aimee, Ms Evans—'

She stopped and turned. 'What do *you* want?'

Eric didn't get a chance to tell her — which was just as well, since nothing had come to him yet. Two women had entered the gym and were hurrying towards the actress.

The larger woman with platinum blonde hair was beaming. 'Aimee, darling, look who's here!'

Aimee turned an expressionless face to the other woman, a petite brunette with large glasses. 'Who are you?'

The petite woman held out her hand. 'Sue Adams, *Teen Time* magazine.'

'She wants to do a story about you, darling!' the other woman said. 'A week in the life of a rising star!'

Aimee didn't look any friendlier. 'I want article approval,' she told the woman. 'Nothing goes into that magazine that I haven't seen and okayed.'

'Not a problem,' Sue Adams chirped. Then she noticed Eric. 'And who might you be?'

'I might be an extra,' he said stupidly. 'I mean, I *am* an extra. My name's Eric Morgan.'

The woman smiled and shook his hand. Aimee then turned to the blonde woman. 'Mom, I'm starving.'

'I've got lots of goodies all ready for you in the trailer, sweetie pie,' the woman said. She linked an arm with Aimee's.

'It was nice to meet you, Eric,' the magazine writer called out before running after them.

Eric watched the three of them leave the gym, but he was mainly watching Aimee. If he imagined that the blonde curly hair was brown and straight, he could be watching Amy Candler. The two girls were the same height, the same shape, and they even had the same walk.

But the similarities pretty much ended there.

8

'She's not your clone,' Eric told Amy.

They were sitting across from each other on the twin beds in Tasha's room, which was always a lot neater and cleaner than Eric's.

'How can you be so sure about that?' Amy wanted to know. 'You told me yourself you barely spoke to her!'

'But I was watching her, and—'

'And she looks just like me, right?'

'Yeah, but she doesn't *act* like you. Amy, this girl is *mean*. You should hear the way she talks to people. She threatened to blackmail the costume woman!'

'You're exaggerating,' Amy declared.

'No, I'm not! I was there, I heard her!'

Amy couldn't doubt his sincerity. 'Okay, but she was probably just in a bad mood. You shouldn't make judgments about people based on one meeting.'

'Look, all I'm saying is that I don't think this girl is related to you.'

Amy got off the bed and went to Tasha's dresser. She stared at herself in the mirror. 'People can be related without being completely alike in personality. Look at you and Tasha! My mother told me that even identical twins can have different personalities.'

In the mirror she saw Tasha come into the room, her gymnastics bag slung across her shoulder. When Tasha saw Eric sprawled on her bed, she was not pleased. 'What are you doing in my room?' she demanded. Then she saw Amy. 'Oh, hi.'

'I just came over,' Amy told her. 'I saw Eric from my window, and I wanted to know about the tryouts.'

'Right.' Tasha tossed her bag on the bed. 'So, what happened?' she asked Eric. 'Did you get a good look at the actress before they threw you out?'

'They didn't throw me out,' Eric said. 'I'm an extra.'

'You're kidding! Tell me!'

He just groaned and fell back on the bed.

'Go on, Eric,' Amy insisted. 'Tell her what you told me.'

'*You* tell her,' Eric muttered.

'*Somebody* tell me!' Tasha sounded irritated.

'Eric said she was nasty,' Amy said.

'Well, we already knew that, didn't we?' The phone rang. Both Tasha and Eric lunged for it.

'My room, my phone,' Tasha yelled. She reached it first. 'Hello?' She listened, and then she made a face. 'It's for you,' she said to Eric. 'Take it in your own room.'

But Eric grabbed it out of her hand. 'Hello? Yeah, this is Eric.' There was a pause. 'Sure, I remember. But why do you want to talk to me?'

Amy tried *not* to hear the voice on the other end of the line. But it wasn't easy – especially since Eric's expression was so odd.

'I don't know,' he was saying. 'I mean, I don't think I can – no, it would be okay with my parents, I guess, but – well, no, not really, but—' He started to look as if he were trapped. 'Uh, can I call you back?' He jotted some numbers down on a pad by the phone. 'Yeah . . . yeah, I'll call you back tonight.'

'Who was that?' Amy asked.

Eric scratched his head. 'You know the writer I told you about? The one who was with Aimee's mother?'

Tasha looked confused. 'You met Aimee's mother? And a writer?'

'A reporter for *Teen Time* magazine,' Amy told her. 'She's doing an article about Aimee Evans. What was her name, Eric?'

'Sue Adams. That was her on the phone.'

'How did she know where to find you?' Amy asked.

'I told her my name, and I guess she got the number from the school.'

'Why did she call?'

Eric looked embarrassed. 'She thinks it would be interesting to write about Aimee going out on a date.'

Tasha's brow furrowed. 'And she wants you to find someone for Aimee to go out with?'

'No. She wants me to be the date.'

Tasha burst out laughing. 'You? She wants you to be Aimee Evans's date? No way!'

Amy wasn't all that surprised. Eric was cute, athletic, and smart. She didn't have any problem envisaging him as an ideal date for any-one.

But Eric did. 'I don't want to do it,' he said. 'That girl gives me the creeps.'

'Eric, you have to do it,' Amy said. 'This is our big chance. You'll be alone with her. You can find out all about her.' Another idea struck her. 'I could meet you guys somewhere, accidentally-on-purpose! And then you could make yourself scarce so Aimee and I could really talk.'

Eric shook his head. 'This Sue Adams will be with us the whole time so she can write about the date. A photographer, too.'

Amy was disappointed. 'Oh, well. But it's still a chance for you to get closer to Aimee. If she likes you, if you two get along, she'll want to meet you again. Then maybe I can meet her too.'

Now Tasha got into the plan. 'And I could meet Sue Adams. Maybe she could get me a job at *Teen Time*!'

'I don't think *Teen Time* magazine hires many twelve-year-olds, Tasha,' Amy murmured.

'I'm a junior reporter for the *Journal*,' Tasha pointed out. 'Why couldn't I be a junior reporter for *Teen Time*?'

'Forget it, both of you,' Eric said. 'I'm not going on a date with Aimee Evans and that's it.'

He sounded like he'd definitely made up his mind. Amy had to think hard and fast.

'Eric . . . remember that maths assignment? The one you said you had to do by next week?'

He eyed her suspiciously. 'Yeah, what about it?'

'You go on the date with Aimee . . . and I'll do the assignment for you.'

Eric was torn. 'For real?'

'For real.'

'What are you talking about?' Tasha asked. 'What maths assignment? How come I don't know about any of this?'

Amy didn't respond. She was busy watching Eric, and she could see the struggle going on behind his eyes. Finally he said, 'Okay. I'll do it.'

Amy clapped her hands in glee.

'But don't forget our other bargain,' he warned her. 'You're still going to watch Ronald Hurley tonight, right?'

'Absolutely,' Amy promised. 'When's your date?'

'Tomorrow night,' Eric said. Amy noticed that his face was taking on a slight greenish tinge as he thought about it.

She jumped up. 'I'm heading over to Ronald Hurley's house right now. I'll call you tonight if I see anything. And you're going to call Sue Adams back, right?'

'Right,' Eric said in resignation.

'Great. See ya later. Bye, Tasha.' She barely heard Tasha's 'Bye' as she ran out the room.

A few hours later Amy had a stroke of luck. She'd gone straight to the Hurley home but had to walk around the block more than a few times before Ronald showed up in the den. At last she spotted him sitting at his desk. And his computer screen was flickering. Quietly, and making sure no one was around to see her, Amy crept closer to the den window.

She'd only played Disaster Isle once, and she didn't know the format well at all. Still, she found that if she concentrated and really strained, the tiny words at the top of the screen came into focus.

DISASTER ISLE: LEVEL FOUR

Eric was going to be ecstatic. She ran home within seconds. And she dialled Eric's number even faster.

When Eric arrived at school early the next morning, he was relieved not to see Aimee among the movie people in the gym. But Sue Adams was there, and she dragged Eric over to meet Aimee's mother.

'This is the boy who will be Aimee's date to-night, Mrs Evans.'

The big blonde woman looked him over. 'Yes, I remember seeing you yesterday. Now, don't get any bright ideas, young man. This so-called date is strictly for publicity purposes. My little Aimee is only twelve years old.' She paused. 'Of course, she's not your ordinary twelve-year-old. But she has no interest in you. And I don't want you to show any special interest in her. If you know what I mean.'

It was the farthest thing from Eric's mind. 'I know what you mean.'

'There's nothing to worry about,' Sue Adams broke in. 'I'll be the chaperone, and they won't have a moment alone. Eric, give me your address, and I'll pick you up at seven.'

The great Aimee came in just then, followed closely by a man struggling to do something to her hair.

'Slow down, slow down,' the man was muttering.

'Move faster,' she snapped.

Sue Adams beamed at her. 'Aimee, I want you to meet Eric Morgan, your date for tonight!'

Aimee gave no sign of recognising him. She scarcely even glanced his way. Eric didn't think it was possible for him to feel more ill at ease until Jeanine and her friend Linda suddenly appeared by his side. 'Hi, Eric! Hello, Aimee!' they chorused.

A voice came through a loudspeaker somewhere. 'Aimee Evans, report to make-up.'

'Gee, you'd think they could at least say "please,"' Jeanine said. Aimee allowed her a brief smile before sauntering off.

'You know what just occurred to me?' Linda mused. 'Aimee looks familiar.' She snapped her fingers. 'Amy Candler! That's who she looks like. Isn't that weird? They even have the same name.'

'Don't be ridiculous,' Jeanine said. 'Aimee Evans is much prettier than Amy Candler.'

The voice came over the loudspeaker again. 'All extras report to the bleachers.' Eric climbed up the bleachers, taking a place behind a guy who was taller so he wouldn't be seen too much. Mr Hardy addressed them.

'Okay, kids, this is what's happening. We're going for reaction shots here. You're watching a basketball game. When someone from your school scores, you cheer. When someone from the other team scores, you boo. When someone from your school just misses a basket, you groan. Got it?'

Someone was confused. 'Where are the players?'

'We're not shooting the game now,' Mr Hardy told them. 'Just the reaction shots from the crowd.'

'Then how do we know when to react?'

Mr Hardy looked pained. 'When I tell you to cheer, you'll cheer. Got it?'

Eric slumped in his seat. Oh well, it was better than answering the roll in homeroom.

Amy was having a hard time concentrating at school that day. It was too easy to let her fantasies drown out the teachers. She was imagining Eric on his date. She was sure Aimee would turn out to be much nicer than they thought. And soon she and Aimee would meet. She was sure of it. And once they met, they'd really bond. They could even search for the other Amys together.

Eric was being sweet. She knew he didn't really want to do this. But she wasn't really asking that much from him. All he had to do was go out on an all-expenses-paid date with a pretty girl. Big deal.

When she went to her English class, she found Jeanine in an exceptionally giddy state, and she wouldn't even let Amy get to her seat before regaling her with her news. 'I've just been called to the set! I'm playing the part of Marcia, and she has a very important scene right at the beginning of the movie with Aimee and Rory!' Jeanine didn't even wait to see Amy's reaction before scampering out of the room.

At least Amy didn't have to fake attention in English. The class was given a pop quiz, which she completed in five minutes. After that she pretended to study her answers while she daydreamed.

'Amy?' The teacher spoke softly. Amy looked up, and the teacher beckoned to her. 'If you've finished the quiz, would you take this message to the office?'

'Sure,' Amy said, and hurried off. The halls were very quiet as she ran the errand. Her ears picked up the faint sound of activity on the floor above her, and she distinctly heard the word *Action*. Checking to make sure no one was around, she tore up the stairs four steps at a time. She stopped abruptly when she reached the hallway.

There was a flurry of activity outside a classroom.

REPLICA

A tall, freestanding lamp shot a bright beam into the room. She spotted Aimee, having her hair combed. A woman was patting make-up onto Rory's face.

Amy slid against the wall, positioning herself so that she could see into the room. Mr Hardy came out. 'This will be a take! Positions, everyone!'

Then she saw Jeanine, lying on her back on the floor of the room. She didn't look happy. Aimee, on the other hand, did. She was watching with a small, satisfied smile on her face. She whispered something to Mr Hardy, and the director called out, 'Facedown!' Jeanine rolled over. Something that looked like the shaft of a knife was carefully placed on her back, and then some sticky red stuff was dripped onto her.

Rory went into the room and stood by Jeanine. Aimee stayed outside the classroom door, and someone placed a stack of books in her arms.

Mr Hardy looked around. Then he yelled, 'Lights! Camera! Action!'

Another voice called, '*Middle School Maniac*, take one.'

Amy watched as Aimee walked into the classroom and almost tripped on Jeanine. She screamed and dropped the books. One of them fell on Jeanine's head, and she twitched.

Mr Hardy was not pleased. 'Don't move, you're suppose to be dead! Okay, take it again.' He watched the action through a camera, and although Jeanine didn't move this time, he still wasn't pleased. 'It's the lighting,' he grumbled. 'You need to work on that. Five minutes, everyone! Dead body, stay there so we don't have to redo the blood.'

As Amy watched, Aimee stepped over Jeanine's body and went into the rest room across the hall. Holding her breath, moving swiftly and silently against the wall, Amy edged down to the rest room door and slipped inside.

Aimee was just coming out of a stall. Her eyes flashed when she saw Amy. 'You again? What are you doing here? What do you want?'

'We need to talk,' Amy said eagerly. 'Please, it's important.'

'Really? I have no interest in talking to you.'

'Why not?'

'Because we have nothing to talk about!' She started past Amy, and Amy threw herself against the door.

'Hey!' Aimee yelled in outrage. 'What do you think you're doing?'

'Look at me,' Amy pleaded. 'Can't you tell that we have something to talk about?'

Aimee's eyes narrowed dangerously. 'I know what you're after.'

'You do?'

'You think you can take my place in this film, don't you? You're trying to get me fired!'

'No! That's not it at all! Aimee, there's a reason we look so much alike!'

The actress stared at her coldly, but at least Amy had her attention.

'Do you – Do you know about yourself? Do you know about us? Do you know what we are?'

Suddenly Aimee pushed her, and Amy was knocked away from the door. She wasn't sure whether Aimee had used unusual strength or she'd just been taken by surprise. She reached out and grabbed Aimee's hand as Aimee reached for the door handle.

'Aimee, listen to me! Can't you feel it? We're alike!'

'There's no one like me!' Aimee hissed.

'Yes, there is – I mean, there are! There are twelve of us!'

Just then the door of the rest room opened.

Aimee's mother stood there. She took one look and screamed.

'Get your hands off my Aimee! Guards! Guards! Help!'

But Amy was long gone before any help arrived.

9

'D on't forget,' Amy told Eric as he combed his hair. 'Check her arm for bruises. I grabbed it pretty hard this afternoon. If she's a regular person, she should have some black-and-blue marks. But if she's a clone, they'll have faded by now.'

'Okay, okay,' Eric said, trying to get an even parting in his hair. Then he presented himself for inspection in the Morgans' living room.

'Shouldn't you be wearing a jacket and tie?' Mrs Morgan asked.

'Sue Adams said I should dress casual,' he told his mother.

'Dressing casual doesn't mean dressing like a slob,' Tasha remarked.

'He doesn't look like a slob,' Amy objected.

Eric didn't think so either. In his khaki pants, UCLA T-shirt, and high-top sneakers, he thought he looked exactly right for the part he was about to play; an average, ordinary ninth-grader going out on a date with a movie star and possible clone.

'Oh my, will you look at that,' said his father, and he wasn't referring to Eric's clothes. The others gathered around him at the window and looked out onto the street.

It wasn't uncommon to see stretch limousines in Los Angeles. But very few came to their condo community on the western fringes of the city. Eric had the awful feeling that half the neighbourhood was looking out their windows and gaping.

'See ya,' he said. He grabbed his denim jacket off the coat-rack by the door and ran out. He couldn't believe his whole family, plus Amy, were going to be watching him get into that fancy car.

It got worse. A man in a uniform got out and opened the back door for him. Eric climbed in next to Aimee Evans.

'Hi,' he said.

She gave him an uninterested glance and looked out the window on her side. He glanced down at her arms. Too bad; she was wearing long sleeves.

Sue Adams turned to him from the front passenger seat, and she was a lot friendlier. 'Hi, Eric! Now, listen, I want you to relax and have fun tonight, okay? Just treat this like any ordinary date.'

Considering the fact that he'd only had three dates in his entire life, he wasn't sure what that meant.

'The photographer will be meeting us at Playland,' she went on. 'Have you ever been there?'

'Sure.' When he was around eight years old, he'd had a birthday party there. He spoke to Aimee. 'Do you like miniature golf?'

She didn't even look at him when she replied, 'Not particularly.'

'Me neither,' he confessed. 'Couldn't we just go to the movies?' He thought he'd prefer to be in a dark place where he was less likely to be seen.

'Miniature golf makes for good pictures,' Sue Adams told him.

When they arrived, Eric discovered that the entire miniature golf course had been rented for their private use. He was grateful that there wouldn't be people staring at this miserable-looking couple followed by a chaperone and a photographer.

They were given clubs and directed to the first hole. Eric vaguely remembered it – a fairly easy one, just a windmill that passed slowly in front of the hole. But he must have been nervous, because it took him two shots to get into the hole.

'Don't worry, we won't print that,' Sue told him. 'Aimee, you know what we want you to do here.'

Aimee grimaced, but she nodded. She took the club and swung. The ball hit the windmill and bounced off. She let out a gasp of dismay. All the while, the camera was flashing.

She couldn't be a clone, Eric thought. Amy would have gotten that shot easily.

'Try to look more embarrassed,' the reporter instructed her. 'Good, good, our readers will identify with that.'

'Okay, but that's the only one I'm missing on purpose,' Aimee told her. 'I don't want to look uncoordinated.'

'We just need one shot like that,' Sue assured her. 'You can try your best for the rest of the game.'

Aimee didn't have to try very hard. For someone who didn't particularly like miniature golf, she was good at it. But so was Eric. Their scores matched, hole for hole.

They barely spoke to each other. Occasionally Sue or the photographer instructed them to put their heads together as if they were talking. Eric had to pose with his arms around Aimee, as if he was showing her how to hold the golf club properly. Another time they had to link arms and pretend to laugh. With each photograph, as soon as the flash faded, so did Aimee's smile.

Eric felt really creepy not making any conversation at all. 'I guess this isn't much fun for you,' he ventured as they walked to a hole.

Aimee shrugged. 'It's a means to an end.'

'What's the end?' he asked.

'My goal.'

'Oh, right. You want to be rich and famous.'

'I want more than that. I want power.' Aimee said it simply, almost as if she were making a comment about the weather. Her tone made him shiver.

But the really scary thing happened at the last hole. The score was tied. 'This will be cute,' Sue said enthusiastically, writing furiously in her little pad. 'No winners, no losers.'

'I always win,' Aimee said.

Eric was getting annoyed. 'Hey, don't be so sure about that,' he said, half-joking and half-serious. 'This is a pretty tough hole.' The ball had to go up a hill, across a creek, and through a blade contraption, where it had to miss being guillotined. The player needed great aim and a powerful swing.

Eric focused on the distant hole. He swung the club back, hard, and started his swing.

'Ow!' he yelled. It felt like a brick had just dropped on his big toe.

'Oh, did I step on your foot?' Aimee asked. 'Sorry. But your club touched the ball, so that counts as a shot.'

He couldn't believe it – she'd stomped on his foot just so she could win this stupid game. His toe was throbbing now, and he thought it might be broken.

Calmly Aimee finished the game, and she posed jumping in the air with glee for the photographer. She flashed Eric something that remotely resembled a smile. 'Like I said, I always win.'

He still wasn't sure if she was a clone or not, but this much he knew: She wasn't like any girl he'd ever met before. Or wanted to meet again.

★ ★ ★

Amy and Tasha had been watching a movie on TV for almost an hour. Amy was glad Tasha seemed to be into it – that gave Amy time to think about her next plan of action. Obviously, she couldn't approach Aimee again if her mother was around. So she'd have to figure out another way to make the girl listen to her . . .

'Isn't Leonardo DiCaprio adorable?' Tasha sighed.

'Oh, sure, he's fabulous,' Amy replied.

Tasha turned to her. 'Amy, Leonardo DiCaprio isn't in this movie. You're not even paying attention to it.'

'I know,' Amy said. 'I guess I've just got too much on my mind.'

Tasha nodded. 'I've got something on my mind too.'

Amy was eager for a distraction, and she knew that something had been bugging Tasha. 'What?'

'You and Eric.'

'What about me and Eric?'

'You're getting awfully close.'

'We've been friends for a while now, if that's what you mean.'

'I think you want to be more than friends,' Tasha said.

Amy fell silent. Then she admitted the truth. 'Well, sort of. Well, I mean . . . yeah.' She turned to her friend. 'Is it bothering you?'

Tasha nodded.

'I'm sorry,' Amy said. 'You know, you're still my number-one best friend. And we've always talked about having boyfriends someday.'

'But not *Eric*,' Tasha moaned. 'Not my brother.'

'Why not? He's not *my* brother. To me, he's a regular boy. A cute boy.'

Tasha looked at her in horror. 'Eric? Cute?'

'Okay, maybe not to you,' Amy said. 'But to me . . . yeah. He's cute.'

'I can't understand it,' Tasha said. 'It gives me the creeps, thinking about the two of you. And don't you dare say I'm jealous.'

'I wasn't going to say that,' Amy told her. 'What I was going to say is, well, if it really bugs you to see me and Eric together, I'll tell him we can't be together.'

Tasha was surprised. 'You'd do that for me?'

Amy nodded. 'I won't be happy about it, but I'll do it.'

Tasha fell silent. 'I guess I can't ask you to do that,' she said finally.

'Whew, that's a relief,' Amy said.

Tasha looked at her curiously. 'Has he ever kissed you?'

'No,' Amy admitted. 'Not yet. I mean, we've never even been on a date.'

Tasha gazed up at the ceiling. 'I wonder if he'll kiss *her* tonight?'

Amy picked up a pillow and tossed it at Tasha.

'Hey,' Tasha cried in outrage, 'watch it! You could suffocate me with that!'

Amy laughed. 'I'm not *that* strong. Or may be I am, I don't know.'

'Let's find out,' Tasha said, grabbing a pillow and throwing it. Soon it was just like old times.

10

Amy heard the heavy slam of the limo door outside. She hit the Pause button on the remote. 'Eric's home,' she told Tasha.

Tasha looked at the clock on her nightstand. 'He hasn't even been gone two hours! Wow, she sure got sick of *him* fast.' The girls scrambled off the bed and ran downstairs.

Eric was sticking his head in the door. He looked around furtively. 'Are Mom and Dad here?' he asked Tasha.

'No, they went out. Why?'

Eric came in. He only had to take one step for the girls to see that something was wrong. 'You're limping!' Amy exclaimed.

Eric made his way slowly to a chair and sank

down. 'I think I've got a broken toe.' He took off his sneaker and sock. Amy knelt down and looked.

'What do you think?' Eric asked her.

'Eric, I'm not a doctor.'

'I just thought that with your powers—'

'I don't have X-ray vision.'

Tasha looked too. 'I don't think there's much you can do for a broken toe, anyway. What happened, exactly?'

'The great movie star stepped on it.'

'And broke your toe?' Amy asked. 'Wow, that's amazing!'

Eric looked at her askance. 'You're happy she broke my toe?'

'No, of course not,' Amy said impatiently. 'Don't you see what this means? If an ordinary person stepped on your toe, it might hurt, but your toe probably wouldn't break. A person would have to be awfully strong to do that.'

'As strong as a clone?' Tasha asked.

'Well, stronger than your average girl. I think *I* could probably break Eric's toe.'

'Let's not try and find out,' Eric said hastily. 'Anyway, you don't have to be *that* strong. There was a boy in my cabin at camp when I was six years old who stepped on the counsellor's foot and broke *two* toes.'

'Tell us about the date,' Amy demanded. 'Everything. Start to finish, don't leave out one detail.'

'That girl,' Eric said, 'may or may not be a clone, but I can tell you this much. She isn't human.'

Amy listened to Eric's tale of his date with the Wicked Witch of the West and took his remarks with a grain of salt. He was a little annoyed when she didn't respond with more sympathy.

'She just hurt your macho pride when she played as well as you did,' she declared.

'Amy, she's *evil!*,' Eric exclaimed. 'You gotta believe me.'

Amy considered this. 'You know, I'm remembering how scared and confused I felt when I first learned what I am. Maybe this is how *she's* dealing with it. Did you notice if she had any bruises on her arm?'

'She was wearing long sleeves. Did you do my maths assignment?'

'Yeah, it's in your room. Eric, are you sure she didn't say or do anything that might prove she's like me?'

'If you were anything like her, you wouldn't be

in this house.' Eric got up. 'I just hope she isn't going to make me lose money.' He hobbled towards the kitchen, and the girls followed him. 'I don't think they're going to want a limping extra in the movie.' He checked the schedule he'd posted on the refrigerator. 'Saturday . . . that's a relief, they don't need me tomorrow. Just the girls.'

'How come?' Amy asked.

'I don't know.' He looked at the schedule again. 'They're supposed to meet at the pool. Maybe it's a girls' swimming class.'

'A swimming class,' Amy repeated. 'Oh, wow!'

'What?' Tasha asked.

'Swimming means bathing suits. If Aimee's wearing a bathing suit, I can see if she has a birthmark like mine!'

'But how are you going to get close enough to have a look?' Eric asked. 'They've got guards protecting the sets.'

'And her mother won't be too thrilled to see you again,' Tasha added.

What they said was true, but Amy didn't let it bother her. 'I'll think of something.'

As it turned out, it wasn't all that hard to get close. There *was* a guard at the gym door. But Amy knew there was a special tutoring programme held on Saturday mornings in the school library, and the main door would have to be open. It didn't take her long to hurry through the building and arrive at the end where the gymnasium and pool were.

She heard voices coming from the physical education office, and the door was ajar. Positioning herself where she could see inside but no one inside would notice her, she counted half a dozen girls, all wearing the navy blue tank suits and white swim caps that the girls at Parkside were required to wear in swimming classes. In these outfits, they all looked alike; but upon closer scrutiny, Amy could see that Aimee wasn't among them. They were giggling as they had their make-up applied by a man dressed all in white, with a white bonnet covering his hair and a white mask covering the lower half of his face. He looked more like a surgeon than a make-up artist.

Amy scurried past the door and ducked into the girls' locker room. There she found the regulation suits, undressed quickly, and put one on. Then she gathered up her hair and pulled a white swim cap over it.

She gave herself a quick once-over in the mirror. She looked just like the others. Turning sideways, she twisted her head so she could see her back. Yes, the small crescent moon was completely visible. If Aimee was here, and if she was wearing the same type of suit, her crescent moon would be visible too. If she had one.

Amy decided it might be best if she went ahead and got into the pool while it was still empty. She could position herself in a corner, stay underwater as much as possible, and hope to blend in with the others when they all came in.

Unfortunately, she wasn't going to be the first in the pool. Through the smoky glass that surrounded the area, she saw that someone was already in the water. She moved closer. With a little concentration, she could see clearly, but it took her a second to absorb what she was seeing.

Someone wasn't just in the pool. Someone was floating facedown.

Aimee Evans! It had to be.

All these thoughts raced through Amy's head in a nanosecond. Then she burst through the doors, ran to the pool, and dived in. She swam to the body, flipped it over, and dragged it towards the edge.

Her heart leaped. Aimee wasn't dead; Amy could feel her moving. No, not moving – thrashing about wildly. Even though Amy's head was underwater, she could hear Aimee yelling. And over that, the sound of a voice shouting, 'Cut! Cut!'

Amy wasn't sure whether her own grip loosened or Aimee broke free on her own. In any case, when she came up for air, she saw Mr Hardy pointing at her. 'Who *is* that? She ruined the shot!' Then Aimee's mother started screaming.

'She's the one who's stalking my daughter! Get her!'

Amy didn't hang around to hear more. She scrambled out of the water and took off. But even as she ran, an image remained in her head. Aimee's right shoulder blade – where there was no crescent moon.

She heard the steps behind her getting closer. There was no time to get her clothes out of the locker room, so she decided her best bet was to hide. When she reached the hall, she realised that no sound was coming from the office where the extras had been getting made up. She ducked in there and crouched low behind a table. Peering out cautiously, she could see the feet of the guards as they ran past the office.

She couldn't risk trying to get out of the room

immediately, so she looked around for a better hiding place. She spotted a large cabinet under a counter and crawled inside. It was a tight fit, but she managed to close the door.

The crack between the door's rim and the wall of the cabinet gave her some light, and she could see into the office. Well, to about one foot above the floor, at least.

A pair of white-clad legs came into the room. She could hear objects being moved around on the counter above her head. A moment later two jeans-clad legs entered.

'You doing my face today?'

She recognised the voice of Rory, the soap-opera actor who had the lead opposite Aimee. The make-up man must have still been wearing his mask, because his response was muffled. 'Yes.'

She heard the creak of the chair as Rory sat down. 'Man, I hate the way you guys wear those masks and caps,' Rory commented. 'Makes me feel like I'm going to have an operation here.'

The man mumbled something about allergies.

'Yeah, I know all about allergies,' Rory said. 'I got about a zillion of 'em. You should a seen me the time I ate strawberries. I broke out so bad I couldn't work for two weeks.'

The man must have asked him something Amy didn't hear, or maybe he'd just pointed to something, because Rory spoke again.

'Naw, that's just a regular ol' zit. You can cover it with that pancake stuff, right?'

The man must have responded in the affirmative, because it was a while before Rory spoke again.

'Can I take a look now?' he asked. 'Very cool; excellent,' he said, obviously examining himself in a mirror. 'I can't even see that hickey on my neck. Thanks, man.'

Rory left the office. Now all Amy had to do was wait for the make-up man to clear out. By now she figured they'd given up looking for her. Everyone had to be in the pool, filming, so she could sneak back into the locker room, pull on her clothes, and get out of the building.

The man was taking his time. Cleaning up, probably, Amy thought. She tried to relax and think about something other than her uncomfortable position in the cabinet.

But all she could think about was Aimee's ordinary back. She wasn't sure how she felt. In a way, she supposed it was a relief. From what she'd seen of Aimee, and from what Eric had told her, she wasn't the kind of girl anyone would want to claim as a sister. But on the other hand, she'd wanted so much to find another like herself.

Was that make-up man never going to leave? Maybe she should just fling open the door and make a dash for it.

But she didn't have to do that. 'You can come out now, Amy.'

She started. How could he know she was in the cabinet? And that voice – it was very familiar.

'Come out of the cabinet, Amy.' The voice was firmer now, more commanding, and she knew where she'd heard it before.

She pushed on the cabinet door and climbed out. She didn't even have to look at the man, who had removed his mask and bonnet, to identify him. Mr Devon.

She'd first met him when he'd pretended to be an assistant principal here at Parkside, and most recently he'd been a doctor at the hospital where her mother had lain in a coma. Now he was a make-up artist for the cast of *Middle School Maniac*.

'How did you know I was in there?' she asked. It

was a dumb question. Mr Devon knew everything. He didn't even bother to answer her.

'This isn't the place for you,' he said.

'What do you mean?'

'Don't get involved in this,' he told her.

Her heart fluttered. 'So she *is* like me! That's why you're here!'

But his next words killed that notion. 'She's nothing at all like you.'

Her heart sank. 'Then you're just here for me. That means the people from the organisation are here too. Who is it? Someone connected with the movie?'

'Just leave,' Mr Devon told her.

Amy wasn't in the mood to be pushed around. She put her hands on her hips and didn't budge. 'I think I have a right to know what's going on.'

Mr Devon's face took on the assistant principal expression. 'Amy, do what I say. Go. Now.'

When she still didn't move, he put a hand on her shoulder and firmly steered her out into the hall. She supposed she could have fought him off, but there was something about Mr Devon that made her reluctant to get physical. After all, he was on her side. At least, that was what she'd always assumed.

The hall was silent. She couldn't hear any sound coming from the girls' locker room. There was no way she was going to leave the building in this disgusting tank suit.

Moving as silently as possible into the locker room, she headed for the bench where she'd left her clothes. She didn't make it.

Hands gripped both her arms, pulling them back tightly.

'Okay, we got her,' a deep voice said. 'Let's go.'

11

A my started to scream.
'Hey, don't do that!' a man yelled, and she
thought she felt a poke in her back. She had to
assume they had a gun. Were there two of them, or
three?

She was still wet from her plunge into the
swimming pool. They threw a towel around
her, over her head, but even so, she was shivering
as the arms pulled her outside the gym. She
struggled, but there was no point. She might be
a lot stronger than an average girl of her size, but
she was still no match for two or three grown men.
Trying not to panic, she considered her escape
options.

'That's a good girl,' one of them said as she

stopped struggling. The comment annoyed her, so she kicked him.

'Whoa!' he yelled in outrage. 'Cut it out!'

Well, what did they expect her to do, let them take her without a fight? But there was no point in wasting her energy. She'd just have to go along with them and wait for the right moment to get away.

The next thing she knew, she was being pushed into a waiting car, and the towel dropped from her head. She could see now, and counted three men, including the driver. She was sitting in the back seat between the other two.

'Did you get the photo?' one of the back seat guys asked the driver.

'Yeah, no problem. It looked good. We should get some serious money for this.'

She tried to make sense of his words. Money? They had to have been hired by the organisation. They were taking her to them. But why did they need a photo?

Maybe they *weren't* from the organisation but knew about it and were planning to hold her for ransom, thinking the organisation would pay a lot for a live clone. They'd use the photo as proof they had her.

'You okay, kid?' the guy on her right asked.

She wasn't surprised by his concern. The organisation would want her in one piece. But she wouldn't give him the satisfaction of an answer.

Then the man on her left spoke. 'So, what does it feel like to be a movie star?'

What? They thought she was Aimee! They thought they were kidnapping Aimee Evans! She tried hard not to let her surprise show on her face. This could only mean one thing. Aimee was a clone, and the organisation wanted her – just like they wanted Amy.

Her head was spinning. One part of her was exhilarated – she'd been right about the actress!

'You too much of a celebrity to speak to us?' one of the guys asked.

'I'm okay,' she murmured. She was trying to think. Should she keep up the pretence and behave like Aimee? But if Aimee didn't know she was a clone, she'd be bewildered by this. 'What's going on here?' she asked, hoping to sound frightened and confused.

'Oh, give me a break,' the other guy said.

Now, what was that supposed to mean?

'You know all about this,' he continued.

So Aimee *did* know what she was. Or maybe these guys just *thought* Aimee knew. Amy wanted more information, but she knew she had to tread carefully if she was going to get any.

'Why are you doing this?' she asked.

The driver looked at her in the rearview mirror. 'You can stop acting, kid. We don't need a performance.' He turned the radio on. The twangy tones of country music filled the car, and the man on her right began to sing along with Garth Brooks. Amy sank back into the seat.

She tried not to be obvious as she moved her head slightly to get a good look at the man who was singing.

He didn't look particularly ominous. He was balding, with a few measly locks of hair combed over his scalp. He wore a red-and-white-checked shirt, and his stomach hung over his belt.

The man on her other side didn't look like a serious bad guy either, more like a teen who hung out on street corners. He was younger, and skinny, with a really bad complexion and a bored look. From his pocket he pulled out a cigarette and lit it. Immediately the car was filled with noxious fumes.

'Do you mind?' Amy asked. She tried to sound as

haughty as she imagined Aimee would sound under the circumstances.

'Oh. Sorry.' The guy rolled his window down slightly and tossed out the cigarette.

Well, that was nice, Amy thought. These guys not only didn't look like gangsters, they didn't act like them either. She tried something else. 'Could you turn the radio down? It's giving me a headache.'

The driver obliged. Then the fat guy offered her a bottle of mineral water. 'Want a drink?'

'No, thank you.' She was floored. She didn't know hoodlums could be this polite. The organisation must have told them to take good care of her.

And if that was true, that meant they wouldn't dare injure her in any way. When they stopped the car, she could make a break for freedom. They'd come running after her, of course, but she had a feeling she might be able to outrun them. The fat one didn't look very athletic, and if the skinny one was a smoker, he couldn't be in very good shape. As for the driver, if she got out of the car while it was still running, he wouldn't be able to jump out and abandon it.

'Jeez, this traffic is a misery,' the driver muttered.

They were stuck in a jam on the freeway and going nowhere. But she couldn't risk jumping out too soon. They were strong enough to hold her down in the car. She had to bide her time and wait for the right moment. She just wished she weren't wearing the awful tank suit.

Cars were moving slowly in the lane to the left, and for a few seconds a police car rolled along next to them. But the kidnappers didn't seem dismayed by this at all. The skinny one yawned. She supposed she could have screamed for the attention of the police, but she didn't.

Maybe she wouldn't even run when the car stopped. Because now she was beginning to wonder about the people who were behind all this. The agency, the organisation, she didn't know what to call them – those were the important ones, not these hired thugs. Getting away from these guys would be easy. Maybe, just maybe, she should go with them, meet the real enemy, and find out what they really wanted from her. Otherwise, the fear and the flight would just go on and on forever, for her, for Aimee, for the ballet dancer, and for all the other Amys out there. If the organisation had a face, if she knew what they were all up against, she'd have a power she didn't have now.

The traffic was moving again. 'Are we late?' the driver asked. 'What time are we supposed to be there, anyway?'

'She said she'd meet us at two,' the skinny one said. He looked at his watch. 'It's one-forty-five now.'

'We're okay,' the driver said. 'It's the next exit.'

She . . . now Amy knew something. One of the faces would be a woman's. She looked out the window as the car moved off the freeway. She knew where they were. It was near the place where she used to take gymnastics. And now they were pulling into the parking lot of an office complex. Her heartbeat accelerated. Was this the headquarters? She'd been in one of those office buildings before. It was the time they'd tried to get her dental X-rays. The so-called dentist had had an office here.

'Where are we meeting this Adams lady?' the fat man asked.

'Third floor,' the driver told him. 'No, wait, it's the fourth. I think.'

The fat man sighed. 'Hope there's an elevator.'

Adams . . . she'd heard that name, just recently

. . . last night, in fact. Sue Adams was the name of the magazine writer who was following Aimee Evans! Was she one of them? Was she just posing as a reporter to get close to Aimee?

'C'mon, kid.' The car had pulled up to the building, and they were all getting out. This was Amy's chance to run, but she'd made up her mind. She got out of the car and went along with the men.

The lobby was empty, just as it had been when she'd come here for the dentist appointment. They went to the elevator, and one of them pressed a button. Amy could feel her adrenaline pumping. She wasn't quite sure what to prepare herself for, but she was ready for whatever she was about to face.

'So, which is it, kid?' the fat man asked. 'The third floor or the fourth?'

The elevator doors opened. 'How should I know?' Amy retorted.

'Aw, come on.' The skinny guy groaned. 'This was supposed to be all organised. You have to know where the hiding place is.' He was holding the elevator doors so they wouldn't close.

Amy was totally bewildered now. 'Hey, *I'm* the one being kidnapped!'

'Right, and we're the kidnappers,' the skinny one said in his bored voice. 'And you're getting kidnapped so you'll get a lot of publicity and your picture plastered in all the newspapers, we know all that. That Adams lady explained it. Now all we need to know is where she's waiting for us.'

For a moment Amy couldn't speak. 'That's what this is all about?' she asked faintly. 'A publicity stunt?'

'Kid, we're not getting paid by the hour; we don't have all day,' the man who drove the car growled. 'Where are we going?' When Amy didn't respond, he looked really irritated. 'What's the matter, can't you hear me under that cap?' He reached over, grabbed the cap, and yanked it off.

The men looked stunned.

'It's not her!' one of them yelled. 'You saw the picture, she's a blonde!'

'But she looks just like her!'

They all looked sick, but Amy felt truly sick. Aimee Evans had plotted her own kidnapping – as a publicity stunt. It would be in all the papers. Once Aimee Evans made the cover of the *National Enquirer* she'd be released. And everyone would know her name. As for Sue Adams, she had only hired these 'kidnappers.' She had nothing to do with the organisation.

Amy walked away from the elevator in disgust. No one tried to stop her.

12

U nfortunately for Amy, being a clone did not
make her capable of hiding her feelings.
Depression was written all over her face. Fortu-
nately, her mother went out with Monica Saturday
night and spent most of Sunday running errands.
When the phone rang, Amy let the machine pick it
up, and she didn't even call Tasha back. She didn't
want to see or talk to anyone.

Aimee Evans might not have been the kind of
person Amy would have chosen as a sister-clone,
but even so, the thought that she had found one of
the other Amys had given her hope. Now that hope
was shattered. Once again she was all alone.

The disappointment was intense. She'd been up
and down ever since she first encountered Aimee,

but this time she was just going to have to accept that Aimee was only the actress she claimed to be, and nothing more. Somewhere, among the billions of people on the face of the earth, eleven other Amys were wandering around. At this moment in time, though, Amy felt pretty sure she wouldn't cross paths with any of them. She knew she was wallowing in self-pity, but she couldn't help it. As far as she was concerned, she was entitled to feel sorry for herself.

She was still full of self-pity at the breakfast table on Monday morning; this time, Nancy noticed. 'What's wrong?'

'That girl, Aimee, the actress I told you about. She's not a clone.'

Nancy smiled sadly. 'Oh, honey, I know that must be a disappointment. How did you find out?'

She wasn't going to tell her mother about the kidnapping. She'd only be scolded for putting herself in potential danger. 'She hasn't got the crescent mark on her back. We all have the same one, right?'

Nancy nodded. 'It was our way of marking you, so there would be some means of absolute identification. The crescent moon becomes visible at puberty.' She reached out and put her hand on Amy's. 'I'm sorry, dear.'

Amy shrugged. 'It's not your fault,' she mumbled. The doorbell rang. 'There's Tasha,' she said, glad to have an excuse to escape her mother's probing and sympathetic eyes. She grabbed her school things and headed for the door.

'Why didn't you call me back yesterday?' Tasha demanded almost before Amy got the door open.

Amy didn't feel like telling the story. 'I had to do something for my mother,' she lied. Luckily for her, Tasha wasn't all that interested in her excuse. She was bubbling over with news of her own.

'Wait till you hear this. I've got an interview with Aimee Evans this morning!'

Amy tried to show some interest. 'How did that happen?'

'I called my contact at the *Journal*, and I told her about wanting to interview Aimee. She made some calls and set it up. I've got an appointment to meet with her over in the phys ed office during home-room.'

'That's nice,' Amy said dully.

'Is that all you can say? Amy, here's a chance for you to make contact with her! Okay, I know her mother might be around, so you'd better not come with me to the interview. But you could give me a note to pass to her.'

Amy shook her head. 'That's okay.'

'But don't you want to know if she's a clone?'

'Not really. I mean, if she's as awful as she seems . . .' Amy let her voice drift off. Tasha was looking at her curiously. She didn't get a chance to pursue the issue, however, because Eric caught up with them.

He too had news. 'I challenged Ronald Hurley to a game of Disaster Isle,' he said. 'The guy couldn't get past level four! That's the last time he'll run around lying about what a master game player he is.' He grinned at Amy. 'And I owe it all to you. I would never have had the nerve to challenge him if I hadn't known his real level. So thanks again.'

'You're welcome,' Amy said. 'Are you turning in the maths assignment today?'

'No, it isn't due until Friday. If I turn it in early, the teacher will just get suspicious.' He looked at her curiously. 'You feeling okay?'

'Sure,' she said, managing a smile. 'What could be wrong?'

He shrugged. 'I don't know.' A moment later he spotted some buddies and ran off to join them. Tasha went back to talking about her interview.

'There's nothing special you want me to ask her?'

'No,' Amy sighed. 'Nothing special.'

When they arrived at school, they separated. Tasha went off for her interview, while Amy went to homeroom. She'd only been in the room a few minutes when she looked up and saw Tasha beckoning to her frantically.

Amy went to the teacher's desk and got permission to use the rest room. Out in the hall, Tasha was in a state of panic.

'I don't know what to do!' she wailed.

'Calm down!' Amy ordered her. 'What happened? Didn't Aimee show up?'

'She showed up, with her mother. And I had just asked her my first question, about why she wanted to be an actress, when the most unbelievable thing happened!'

Amy had a feeling she knew what was coming, but she let Tasha tell the story.

'Her mother left the room for a minute. Suddenly these two masked guys burst into the room! They grabbed Aimee's arms and pulled her out of the office. The poor girl was so shocked, she didn't even scream!'

'I'll bet,' Amy said. 'Sounds like a kidnapping.'

'Exactly! Then her mother came back and I told her what happened.' Tasha frowned. 'You know, for someone whose daughter was just kidnapped, she didn't seem very upset. She just told me to go away, that she'd call the police and take care of everything.'

'The two men who took her . . . was one of them fat and balding? And the other skinny with a bad complexion?'

Tasha was taken aback. 'How did you know?'

Well, at least the two hired thugs had been given a second chance. 'It was just a publicity stunt.' She told Tasha about her experience the day before.

Tasha was horrified. 'That's terrible!' she exclaimed. 'They're going to have police out searching for her, and there hasn't even been a crime!' She was really angry. 'You know, if someone gets robbed or killed or something today because there aren't any police around, it will be all her fault!'

'I think it's that reporter who set the whole thing up,' Amy said. 'I guess she figures it will make a more interesting story for her stupid magazine.'

Tasha sniffed. 'Well, that's the last time *I'm* going to read *Teen Time*. And I used to think that was a pretty good magazine!'

'Me too,' Amy admitted. 'At least it had some interesting stuff in it, not just the usual articles on how to apply mascara and get a boyfriend.'

'Maybe *Teen Time* doesn't know they have such a sleazy reporter on staff,' Tasha fumed. 'I feel like calling the magazine right now and exposing her unethical tactics.'

'You could do that,' Amy said without much interest. 'I'd better get back into class.'

'So that's why her mother wasn't upset; she must have known about the plan,' Tasha said. She shook her head in annoyance. 'I was more upset than she was! I thought those guys might be a couple of creeps from that organisation that's been after you.'

'Nah, they're just a couple of hired hands,' Amy told her. 'Besides, she's not a clone anyway.'

Tasha stared at her. 'But she has the mark.'

'What did you say?'

'She was wearing one of those whatchamacallit strapless things, like the top part of a gown.'

'A bustier,' Amy said.

'Yeah, that's what it's called. Personally, I

thought it wasn't very appropriate for eight o'clock in the morning. Not to mention the fact that she doesn't have the chest to hold it up. Anyway, she was practically naked.'

'You could see her back?'

Tasha nodded. 'She's got a mark just like yours, a little crescent moon on her right shoulder blade. And I mentioned it before we started the interview, just to see how she reacted. I said, "That's a nice tattoo." '

'What did she say?'

'She told me it wasn't a tattoo, it was a birthmark. In fact, she even said something about wanting to get it removed.' Tasha's brow furrowed. 'Wait a minute. Didn't you just tell me she was wearing a bathing suit on Saturday? How come you didn't see the mark?'

'I don't know . . .' And then she *did* know.

Mr Devon had used special make-up to cover Rory Keller's acne and love bite. There was no reason why a glob of that stuff couldn't also cover the mark of a crescent moon. 'Ohmigosh,' she whispered.

Unaware of the direction of Amy's thoughts, Tasha tried to reassure her. 'Even so, they couldn't have been from the organisation. Otherwise, they would have held on to you Saturday. You're just as valuable to them as she is.'

'But those two jerks didn't know that! They bought that story about a publicity stunt. They were told to get Aimee Evans.' Amy gnawed on a fingernail and tried to think. 'It's that Sue Adams – *she's* from the organisation.'

'Maybe, maybe not,' Tasha cautioned. 'This really could have nothing at all to do with Aimee being a clone.' But the anger on her face had been replaced by worry. 'Well, if she's a real clone, I guess she'll be able to fight them off.'

Amy was chewing her fingernails. 'But if she doesn't know what she is, and what she can do . . . Oh, Tasha, she must be so scared right now.'

'What can we do about it?'

There was only one thing to do. 'You got a piece of paper?'

Tasha tore one out of her notebook. Quickly Amy scrawled the address of the office building where she'd been taken yesterday. 'Get Eric and meet me there. Don't come in, just wait outside.'

'What are *you* doing?'

Amy didn't take the time to tell her. Thank

goodness no one else was in the corridor at that moment. She sped down the hall at a pace faster than any normal girl – or any normal human, for that matter.

13

A my couldn't wait for a bus that might take ages to come. She had to run.

Taking side roads, where she'd be least likely to meet anyone, she sprinted along street after street in a flash. Everything went by in a blur. The few people who did cross her path did double takes, but Amy barely noticed. She was moving like the wind, and with definite purpose.

Shooting onto the freeway, Amy watched for a truck with an open back. She wasn't sure if her skills were strong enough to rely on, but she had to try. Luckily, her running and jumping talents were even better than she'd thought.

What was not so lucky was the fact that the truck she'd chosen was loaded with live chickens in cages.

By the time the truck neared the right exit, she knew she stank to high heaven. Oh well, for once she didn't care about offending anyone. If Sue Adams turned out to be who Amy suspected, she deserved to get a whiff of this.

When the truck reached the exit ramp, Amy took a deep breath, then made a flying leap. She landed on a grassy bank by the side of the highway. She didn't look behind her, but she gave a silent prayer of gratitude when she didn't hear any cars crashing as a result of drivers stunned by the sight.

She reached the office building just a few minutes later, and ran up the stairs. She located the door that she'd once thought led to a dentist's office. There was no sign on it now.

The door wasn't locked. She opened it slowly.

She remembered this reception area. There had been a bogus secretary and patients waiting to see the 'dentist' during her first visit, but the room was empty now. She heard movement in the inner office, and then a voice. 'Sue? Are you back?' A second later Aimee appeared in the doorway. 'You! What are you doing here?'

'Don't get upset,' Amy said quickly. 'I'm here to help you.'

146

'Help me?' Aimee uttered a short, hard, ugly laugh. 'I don't need your help! Just get out of here, okay? And don't tell anyone you saw me.' She came towards Amy, threatening to push her out of the room if she didn't leave willingly.

'No, wait, you have to listen to me, we don't have much time! Where's Sue Adams?'

'Why?'

'Just tell me, where is she?' The urgency in Amy's voice must have gotten through.

'She's getting some food, but she's coming right back. And you'd better not be here when she does.'

'Neither should you. Aimee, I have to tell you—'

Aimee had turned her back on her, and now Amy could see the crescent moon. Her heart leaped.

But Aimee was heading back towards that inner office, and for all Amy knew, she was about to lock herself inside. She had to think fast.

'Look! Can you do this?' Amy grabbed a chair from the waiting room and gave a swift kick to one of its legs. It flew off.

Aimee actually seemed mildly impressed. 'Is that karate?'

'No, it's something I can do because I'm stronger

than other girls. You can do it too. Here, try it!' She offered another chair to Aimee, who looked at her suspiciously.

'What is this, some kind of trick?'

'It's no trick. Haven't you ever noticed that you're stronger than other people? Can see better, hear better? Run faster, jump higher?'

She thought she saw a flicker of recognition in Aimee's eyes. Then she thought of something Aimee could definitely relate to. 'Are you always amazing your directors with how fast you learn your lines?'

Aimee's eyes widened. 'How did you know that?'

'Because you're just like me. We're both in danger and we have to get out of here, *now*.'

Aimee had regained her composure. 'Are you crazy? I'm not going anywhere with you!'

Amy knew that demonstrations of strength weren't going to convince her clone. She took a deep breath. 'Okay, just listen. I'm going to talk fast because there isn't much time.' For a second she hesitated, not sure where to begin. Then she just plunged in.

'Thirteen years ago there was a scientific experiment in cloning. Genetic material from a variety of sources was manipulated and duplicated in an effort to create the ultimate human. It was called Project Crescent. You have a crescent moon on your right shoulder blade. So do I. Look!' She pulled at the neck of her T-shirt and showed Aimee.

Aimee looked, but she didn't say anything, so Amy continued. 'The scientists thought they were doing something for the good of humanity. But they found out that the organisation funding the project was trying to create a master race—'

Aimee interupted. 'Why?'

'To take over the world,' Amy said impatiently. 'That's not important. What's important is that the scientists figured this out in time. They destroyed the project, they blew up the lab, and the organisation thought the clones were blown up too.' She paused. This was the hardest part. 'But the clones weren't destroyed. They still exist.'

Aimee's mouth fell open.

'*We're* those clones, Aimee. You and I. Two of them, at least. There are others. And that organisation – they're looking for us. Whatever it was they wanted to use us for, they still do.'

It wasn't much of an explanation, but that was all

there was time for. Unfortunately, it wasn't enough for Aimee. Without any warning, she came up to Amy and shoved her hard. 'You're crazy. Get out of here.'

The push took Amy by surprise, and she stumbled backwards. 'Aimee, please—'

Aimee pushed her again. This time Amy held firm. She grabbed Aimee's wrist. 'Come on, we have to get out of here.'

An ordinary person wouldn't have been able to break Amy's grip. But Aimee wasn't an ordinary person. She wrenched her arm back and got herself free. Then she stared at her arm, as if not quite believing that she'd done that.

'You see? You see?' Amy said. 'You're not like other people!'

Suddenly Aimee lunged. She grasped Amy by the shoulders and started pulling her towards the door that led out of the office. Amy jerked one arm free and grabbed Aimee's wrist. The struggle began in earnest.

If Amy had any doubts left about Aimee's nature, they soon disappeared. The actress was as strong as she was. Aimee was able to resist Amy's attempts to pin her down, and boy, could she hit! When she pulled at Amy's hair, Amy felt like she was about to lose her scalp. And when Aimee managed to get her hands around Amy's throat, Amy thought she might lose consciousness. She had to use every ounce of her strength to defend herself – something she'd never really had to do before. But then, she'd never fought another clone, someone who was as strong and quick as she was.

Still, it wasn't a completely even fight. Aimee clearly didn't care whether she injured Amy, so her approach was vicious. On the other hand, Amy didn't want to hurt the actress. She also knew her body, its capabilities, and Aimee didn't. Aimee was meaner. Amy was quicker.

They were on the floor, rolling around in a wild struggle to dominate, when Sue Adams returned. The reporter dropped the bag of groceries she was carrying. 'What's going on here?' she cried out.

'Get her off me!' Aimee screamed.

Sue Adams grabbed Amy by the arm. Amy pulled away so hard that the woman was knocked backwards. At that moment the reporter got a real look at Amy's face. She froze. Amy quickly started dragging Aimee towards the exit.

But the reporter's immobility didn't last. 'Stop where you are. Now.'

Something about her tone made Amy look over her shoulder. Sue Adams had a gun, and it was pointed right at her.

Amy loosened her grip, and Aimee broke free. 'She just burst in here, with this wild story! She's nuts!' But Sue Adams wasn't even looking at Aimee. She strode over to Amy and yanked at the neck of her T-shirt. The shirt ripped, revealing Amy's crescent mark.

Sue Adams sucked in her breath sharply. 'Another one,' she whispered.

'What are you talking about?' Aimee demanded.

Amy took advantage of the reporter's shock. Quickly she kicked the gun out of Sue Adams's hand. In her effort to hold on to it, the woman's head got in the way; she went crashing to the floor and lay still.

Aimee stared at her, then turned to Amy. 'Is she dead?'

'No, she's just unconscious.' Amy picked up the gun gingerly. Aimee was watching her, incredulous.

'It's – It's true,' she said finally. 'You were telling the truth.'

'Yes. Now come on, she's not going to stay unconscious forever.'

'Why don't you just kill her?'

Aimee's matter-of-fact tone caught Amy off guard. 'What?'

'You've got the gun. Kill her.'

This wasn't the time to discuss ethics. 'No. Come on, let's get out of here.'

Tasha and Eric were waiting outside the building. Eric wasn't very happy. 'I hope you realise this is going to get me about fifty years of detention.'

'Yeah, but you'll never have to do any maths homework again,' Amy told him hurriedly. 'Look, we can't hang around; there's no telling who could be watching this building. I want you to take Aimee to school. She'll have to pretend she's me.'

'Why?' Aimee wanted to know.

'It's the best way for you to hide. Like I said, we don't know who else from the organisation is around.'

'And where are you going?' Eric asked.

'I'll go to school too. To the movie set. I'll be Aimee.' She turned to Aimee. 'What are you supposed to be doing today?'

Aimee still looked dazed. 'Scene twelve.'

'Is there a script in your trailer?'

Aimee nodded.

'But what about your hair?' Tasha asked. 'And what about Aimee's hair? People are going to notice.'

Amy considered this. 'Put Aimee's hair up and cover it with a baseball cap,' she instructed them. 'Take your make-up off, Aimee. And Tasha, get her some other clothes.' She eyed Aimee's bustier. 'No one could ever believe I would wear something like that. As for *my* hair . . . I don't know . . .'

For once Aimee provided some help. 'There's a wig in my trailer. For when I'm having a bad hair day.'

Aimee provided more assistance − she was the only one among them who had enough money to take a taxi. They stopped at Amy's for clothes and a baseball cap, and Amy thanked her lucky stars that this was one of Nancy's teaching days. And then they went to school.

Aimee wasn't saying much. She still seemed a little out of it, and Amy couldn't blame her. She had to be feeling pretty overcome by all that had happened and all that she had just learned.

'Take her to the infirmary,' Amy advised Tasha. 'Tell the school nurse it's cramps or something. She'll give her an aspirin and leave her alone. As soon as I'm finished with the scene, I'll leave school and come home. Bring her back there when school lets out.'

'Then what?' Eric wanted to know.

'Then? I don't know.'

There was no guard in front of Aimee's mobile home. Amy went inside and found the wig. She also located the script and read scene twelve. In a minute she had it memorised. The wig was a bigger problem. She got it on her head, but she looked really stupid.

There was an even bigger problem outside. She'd completely forgotten about Aimee's mother. The woman was coming towards the mobile home at that very moment. When she saw Amy, she went rigid.

'What – What—' she stammered.

Amy didn't waste time being polite. 'It wasn't a publicity stunt. Sue Adams was really kidnapping Aimee. Don't worry, she's safe. I can't explain now.' She left Mrs Evans standing there gaping and ran to the school's gym entrance. Just before entering, she thought of the school's regulations regarding weapons. She took the gun out of her bag and dropped it in a sewer.

Then she went to the phys ed office for her make-up.

Mr Devon wasn't surprised to see her. But he wasn't pleased.

'You shouldn't have done that, Amy. We would have taken care of it.'

'But it's okay now,' Amy said. 'She's safe.'

'*She's* safe. But no one else is.'

'What do you mean?'

Just then Rory walked in. Quickly Mr Devon applied Amy's make-up, and then Rory's, without saying another word. Then he left the office.

'Strange guy, huh?' Rory commented.

'No kidding,' Amy said with feeling.

The scene they were shooting was a simple one, a conversation between Marco and Amanda, the two main characters, in a classroom. As they took their positions, Amy was feeling pretty good. She knew her lines, and no one had spotted the fact that she wasn't Aimee.

'Scene twelve, take one,' Mr Hardy called out. 'Action!'

'You have to believe me, Amanda,' Rory said. 'I

didn't kill that girl. I've never killed anyone. My brother's death was an accident.'

'I believe you, Marco,' Amy said. 'I'll tell you why. I know that deep down inside, you are a good person. And there's another reason why I believe you. I could never love a killer.'

'Cut!' Mr Hardy yelled. 'Aimee, what's the matter with you?'

Amy looked at him surprised. 'What do you mean?'

'That's the worst reading I've ever heard in my life! Do it again! Scene twelve, take two. Action!'

'You have to believe me, Amanda. I didn't kill that girl. I've never killed anyone. My brother's death was an accident.'

'I believe you, Marco. I'll tell you why. Because I know that deep down inside, you are a good person. And there's another reason why I believe you. I could never love a killer.'

They didn't get any further. 'Cut!' Mr Hardy shouted again. He looked angry. 'Aimee, are you screwing up on purpose?'

Amy was completely bewildered. Was it possible that she had memorised the wrong scene? 'What am I doing wrong?' she asked.

'You're not *acting*!' Mr Hardy practically screamed. 'You're talking in a monotone, you've got no expression, and you sound like a robot!'

'I do?' Amy asked uncertainly. It had never occurred to her that acting would require anything more than learning lines.

'Do it again. And do it right!'

She tried. But Mr Hardy wasn't any more pleased with the third take. Or the fourth, or the fifth . . . and by the time they reached the tenth take, he was livid.

'I don't know what kind of game you're playing,' he said. 'But I'm fed up with it. Are you going to do this right or not?'

'I'm trying,' Amy said. 'I'm doing the best I can.'

He glared at her, long and hard. 'That's the best you can do?'

Amy nodded.

'You won't be able to do this scene any other way?'

Amy shook her head.

'Then you're fired.'

A gasp went up from the cameramen, the prop person, and all the other people on the set. 'But – But—' Amy didn't know what to say.

A grim smile appeared on Mr Hardy's face. 'You've been nothing but trouble since the day you were hired. You're a good actress when you want to be, but I've had enough of your spoiled ways. And I'm not bribing you with another raise. You're not in this movie anymore. We'll get a new actress, we'll reshoot, and *Middle School Maniac* will be a better movie. Get off the set.'

Amy looked at Rory. He just shrugged. 'That's showbiz.'

'Call the casting department,' Mr Hardy told one of his assistants. 'Take an hour break for lunch, everyone. Clear the set.'

Within seconds everyone was gone. And Amy felt worse than she'd felt an hour earlier, when she'd been facing a gun.

14

How was she going to break this news to Aimee? The girl had already received enough in the way of shocking news that day. Now Amy was going to have to tell her she was out of work. And that it was Amy's fault.

Looking out the window, she saw Mr Hardy talking to Aimee's mother in front of the mobile home. She didn't dare go there.

Leaving the classroom, she went directly to a rest room. She took off the wig and washed the makeup off her face. She didn't rush. She wasn't in any hurry to talk to Aimee. Here she was trying so hard to win the girl's trust. Had she caused irreparable damage to their relationship? Would Aimee ever forgive her?

Yes, she told herself. *We're sisters. She may act mean and nasty, but she can't be that bad, not if we're made out of the same stuff. It's her environment that's made her bad. She'll be okay. Just like me.*

Classes were in session, and the halls were quiet. She went directly to the infirmary. The nurse wasn't at her desk. Amy went into the little room with the cots, where students who weren't feeling well could lie down.

The room was empty.

Amy stood there, puzzled. Had Tasha and Eric come up with a better place to hide Aimee? Or maybe she was in one of Amy's classes right now, using her acting skills to be Amy.

'She's gone.'

Amy whirled around.

'She's gone,' Eric repeated.

'Gone where?'

'I don't know. She's just . . . gone.'

Amy sank down on a cot. Eric sat down on the one facing hers.

'Tasha and I were bringing her here. She stopped at a rest room. When she didn't come out, Tasha went in. Aimee had crawled out the window.'

'But why?'

'I don't know.' He put a hand in his pocket and pulled out a folded paper. 'Tasha found this in the rest room. You'd better read it.'

Amy unfolded the paper.

You didn't really expect me to hang around, did you? I suppose I should thank you for clueing me in on what I am, but I would have found out eventually. Now I have to figure out what I can do with myself. I've always wanted power, and now I've got the means to get it. I'm not sure yet how I'll use it, but I'll find a way.

Tell Hardy I won't be in his stupid movie. And if you see my mother, tell her not to miss me. I won't miss her.

And one more thing. Stay out of my way.

Amy crumpled the paper silently. Now she knew why Mr Devon had been so displeased with her. She had just set something evil loose in the world.

'It's not your fault,' Eric said softly. 'You couldn't have known Aimee Evans was really bad.'

Amy sat very still. 'I wonder . . . ,' she said finally.

'You wonder what?'

'If they're all like that. All the other Amys.'

Eric took her hand and squeezed it. 'I'm just glad you're the Amy you are.' After a moment he added, 'Oh, by the way, I tore up that homework you did for me.'

'You did?'

'Yeah. I was using you, and it wasn't right. I'll never ask again, I promise.'

She managed to give him a small smile. 'Okay.'

Eric got up and sat down again right next to her. They sat that way in silence, side by side, holding hands, for what seemed like a long time.

The silence was broken by the voice of the school nurse. 'What are you two doing in here? Are you sick? Do you have notes from your teachers?'

Amy and Eric shook their heads.

The nurse frowned. 'Then you're both in trouble. Go to the principal's office, right this minute.' She pointed to the door and then stood watching them to make sure they went into the principal's office.

'My first detention,' Amy moaned.

'It's not that bad,' Eric assured her. He even grinned. 'And at least we're in it together.'

Memo from the Director

ALL SUBJECTS HAVE BEEN IDENTIFIED AND ARE
UNDER OBSERVATION.
IT HAS BEEN PROPOSED THAT A GROUP ANALYSIS
WOULD BE MORE USEFUL THAN INDIVIDUAL STUDIES.
APPROPRIATE ACTION WILL BE TAKEN.

Collect the Replica series!

Book 1: Amy, Number 7

Amy Candler knows she's different. In fact, she's not Just different, she's perfect!

Suddenly she can and hear things over huge distances. She can perform somersaults like an Olympic gymnast. And she knows the answer to *every* question her teachers ask!

But there's one question Amy can't answer. Why is her past so mysterious? Why can't she find out where she was born? All Amy knows is that her recurring nightmare seems to be telling her something, and that a crescent-shaped birthmark on her back has only just appeared there . . . And weirder still, someone is sending her anonymous warnings to keep her 'special' talents a secret.

Slowly Amy is piecing together her identity – but she'd better hurry – time is running out . . .

Collect the Replica series!

Book 3: Another Amy

Amy Candler knows she's different. In fact, she's not Just different, she's perfect!

Now that Amy has discovered exactly who she is – she needs some more answers, and she needs to share her thoughts with somebody. Not being able to talk to her best friend, Tasha, doesn't help – and now that her mum has a new boyfriend, Amy doesn't want to worry her . . .

But as soon as Amy finds the one person who really understands, she puts his life in danger. And from that point on Amy feels she can't trust anybody – even the people close to her . . .

If only Amy hadn't ignored the warnings not to be perfect . . . .

REPLICA
Marilyn Kaye

0 340 74951 2	Amy, Number 7	£3.99	☐
0 340 74952 0	Pursuing Amy	£3.99	☐
0 340 74953 9	Another Amy	£3.99	☐

All Hodder Children's books are available at your local bookshop, or can be ordered direct from the publisher. Just tick the titles you would like and complete the details below. Prices and availability are subject to change without prior notice.

Please enclose a cheque or postal order made payable to *Bookpoint Ltd*, and send to: Hodder Children's Books, 39 Milton Park, Abingdon, OXON OX14 4TD, UK. Email Address: orders@bookpoint.co.uk

If you would prefer to pay by credit card, our call centre team would be delighted to take you order by telephone. Our direct line *01235 400414* (lines open 9.00 am–6.00 pm Monday to Saturday, 24 hour message answering service). Alternatively you can send a fax on *01235 400454.*

TITLE		FIRST NAME		SURNAME	

ADDRESS	
DAYTIME TEL:		POST CODE	

If you would prefer to pay by credit card, please complete:
Please debit my Visa/Access/Diner's Card/American Express (delete as applicable) card no:

Signature . . . . Expiry Date . . . .

If you would NOT like to receive further information on our products please tick the box. ☐